I0705871

Nyifie Brothers Publishing

Copyright © 2024 by Sterling & Stone
This edition published by Johnny B. Truant and Nyfie Brothers
Publishing.
All rights reserved.

No part of this book may be reproduced in any form or by any electronic or
mechanical means, including information storage and retrieval systems,
without written permission from the author, except for the use of brief
quotations in a book review.

Thank you for supporting my work.

GAME OF FANGS

A FAT VAMPIRE PREQUEL

JOHNNY B. TRUANT

ONE

NEW JERSEY

The fifth time JJ broke his neck, he decided maybe his mother had been right about Arek.

Mom was still alive — 101 years old and living with his sister, Olive. From what JJ could see through the window, Mom was as sharp as ever. Not as mobile as she'd been, of course, but whenever JJ allowed Olive to remember who he was, Olive told him Mom's doctor said she might live another ten years. It was starting to seem like Mom might outlive him. It wasn't supposed to be that way — especially given the circumstances — but then again Mom still had something to live for. Hope could take you a long way. Hopelessness, not so much.

JJ tried to be a good son. He'd call more, but Mom didn't have her own phone. To reach her, had to call Olive, then talk his way to the senior lady of the house. But on the phone, there was no way to release the glamours — not the one on Olive, not the one on their mother. That meant he had to pretend to be someone else, hoping an interaction as strangers would be good enough: *Hello, Mrs. Paloma? Have you considered installing ThermoSave windows? No? Well then, how's your health? How's the family? Do you miss your son? Oh, you don't have a son? Well, then, let's try an exercise — strictly for window-selling reasons, of course. If you did have a son, and if his name was JJ, do you think you'd miss him?*

It was depressing. He tried luring Mom to the window, but Mom was mostly deaf (couldn't hear him tapping) and had crippling arthritis that wouldn't let her come to the window anyway. So JJ tried the front door. His plan was to release Olive's glamour, allow her to recognize him, then ask to be invited inside. Olive would do it, too; she knew JJ's secret even though it scared her. He'd had to glamour her because she got nightmares, but that was no problem; JJ could drop her amnesia like a porn star's robe.

It should have worked, but Olive was renting her home. That meant she *couldn't* invite him inside because the force governing vampires seemed to have decided it wasn't actually her house. He'd have to track down the landlord and glamour *him* into an invitation. JJ was willing to try, but even under glamour Olive's landlord hadn't remembered her. He owned hundreds of units, remotely managed, and didn't know his tenants. Would the nice young man mind driving to Lone Star Rentals and asking for Pauline? Pauline could tell him which home his sister was renting.

In the end, it just wasn't worth it. Even if he got inside, Mom would ask why her eldest looked fifty years younger than his sister, and JJ had no good answer. The only way around it was to visit her with her glamour still in place, but that felt a little like giving his own mother dementia.

These days, JJ seldom bothered. Running the 220 miles to visit took at least a half hour, and of course he'd then have to run back — all just to peek through a window with no real hope of interaction. Even unglamouring Olive for a chat wasn't worth it. Olive would be 78 this year, and repeat glamouring and unglamouring had a way of softening human brains. It was best if he just left her alone, believing herself to be an only child. Best for her, but not so great for JJ.

Almost fifty years ago now — when JJ had been 32 and Mom had been 52 — Mom had told him, *That young man Arek is a bad influence on you.* Arek had been 56 at the time, though ironically not as reckless as today. If only Mom could see how he'd turned out. That would really put the nail in the all-too-literal coffin.

"Come on, pussy," Arek was telling JJ now. "Put your back into it!"

"It hurts," JJ told him.

"Please. You've hurt worse."

Which wasn't even a good comeback. That particular response didn't do anything to negate the chief complaint: that repeatedly using your head as a battering ram was uncomfortable and the ram would very much like to stop, please. Hearing such things, Arek did what he usually did: He one-upped JJ like they were a pair of chest-thumping frat boys. At first JJ had gone along with it because the transformation created its own adrenaline, but after a few years the newness went away and JJ had returned to a state of quieter, less intrusive hormones. Unfortunately, although JJ's body would forever be 32, Arek's would forever be 26. Arek was pumping more testosterone than JJ and always would. The result was strange: JJ chronically wishing his 105-year-old maker would grow the hell up already — but if it hadn't happened yet, chances were it never would. When Arek turned five hundred, he'd still be seeking keggers and college girls and winning arguments by calling people "pussy." It was an intolerable situation. JJ, with his more mature biochemistry, sometimes just wanted to sit at home and watch reruns of *Supermarket Sweep*. Death to the undead, but long live the 80s.

Again JJ rammed the door at Arek's command. Behind it, if the home's blueprints were correct, was an old root cellar — probably dirt-floored given the age of the house. Given the state of the owner (a white-haired lady named Elia Sesh), it had probably been stuffed full of homemade jams and jellies before the whole works had been sealed against radon — or, in the likely event she'd forgotten to clear it out first, was *still* full of those things. It was the kind of cellar that kids, visiting grandma, would be afraid to enter. They'd see the shadows of unholy creatures beneath the door and imagine black things scuttling inside: rats, spiders, insects with too many legs. Truth be told, for some of the same reasons, JJ wasn't too keen to enter. Not that he planned on mentioning his nerves to Arek.

"You could help me," JJ suggested.

Arek laughed. "Please. *You're* used to smashing heads."

"I wasn't a lineman. I was a wide receiver. Look at me, will you?"

Not that it was necessary. A lineman would never have been allowed. Every vampire JJ met looked like a wide receiver or a quarterback — one with a perfect face. Or a GQ model. Or a Victoria's Secret model. Recently the trend had been toward Crossfit badasses. Just ... no fatties. No uglies. Nothing but primo physical specimens in Logan's Vampire Nation.

"Yeah," Arek said, "and *I* fought a war. How about a little gratitude? A little 'Thank you for your service'?"

"I wasn't even alive then."

Arek scoffed. "So what? Think it doesn't affect you? Listen, dick. If we hadn't won World War I, the world would have been teed right the fuck up for the Nazis. It wouldn't even have been *close* in World War II. You'd be saluting the swastika right now."

There was no point arguing. JJ was pretty sure that losing the first war was what pissed Hitler off and gave him his start, but Arek wouldn't want to hear that. Winning the first war might have been the worst thing to happen to the Jews, if you ignored everything else.

JJ again slammed the door like a battering ram, and again his neck broke. The hit snapped his cervical vertebre and must have severed his spinal column in the process because as with the last five tries, he collapsed to the ground unable to move, then promptly soiled himself.

"Jesus," said Arek. "Do I need to call a locksmith?"

"I'd settle for a reciprocating saw. Seriously. Glamour the neighbor and ask if he has one."

But Arek, because he was an asshole, thought JJ's suggestion was rhetorical. It was not. A saw would open a wooden door better than a used-to-be-human head and shoulders. Ask anyone at Home Depot and they'd tell you the same.

Still healing, JJ could only watch his maker walk out of view. He couldn't turn his head to follow. All these break-ages were nauseating him — something that had to be psychological because a physical cause would heal with the rest of him. What would happen if he vomited right now, looking up at Grandma Moses's ceiling? Was it possible to drown in your own barf? JJ thought it was — for humans, if not for him.

JJ's dream of death evaporated as a snap announced the repair of his vertebrae. Sensation and movement returned to his body inch by inch. He could feel his chest, then his arms, then his legs, then the shit in his pants. Fully healed, he sat up.

"There must be a wall behind this door or something," said Arek, examining it. "Otherwise a strapping young man like you would be able to break right through." His palm was flat on the door, dreaming of what he hoped was inside. Mrs. Sesh didn't have a key to this particular lock; they'd glamoured her to find out, and then Arek had additionally glamoured her to dress like a Teletubby for the rest of her life. He was a real cock that way.

JJ got to his feet and came to stand beside his maker. The wood had cracked after all of JJ's hits, but the cellar remained impenetrable. According to Mrs. Sesh, her son had hired a firm for "radon mitigation" before dying in a car crash ... but radon mitigation was done with fans and caulk, not cinder blocks. The measures he'd taken frustrated JJ but encouraged Arek: *Why would Daniel Sesh have sealed it so well if he wasn't trying to keep something important — something too powerful for any human nerd to understand — inside?*

"Look," said Arek, lowering his gaze.

JJ's last charge had knocked away a section of mortar to the door's left, beside the knob. Behind it was smooth gray, not more brick. JJ reached out, but Arek grabbed his wrist.

"Easy. I think that's silver."

"There's no way he installed a silver door," JJ said. They'd done their research on Daniel Sesh and knew him to be penniless — sixteen grand a year, tops, working part-time as a grocery bagger at the A&P. He'd lived with his mother, taking over home duties as the old woman grew weak and forgetful. Now the weak and forgetful woman was the only one left. She lived her whole life in front of the living room TV, oblivious to her son's dark hobbies.

"He *didn't* install a silver door," said Arek, carefully peeling back trim and mortar to reveal more gray. "He installed a silver *vault*."

"That'd cost ..." JJ shook his head. "I don't know *what* it'd cost."

Arek stepped back, looking at the partially-opened wall as if it'd bit him.

"What?"

"I think this might be a Lowrider Box."

JJ looked more closely. "Then it couldn't have been *installed*. It'd have to be original — installed when the house was built. How old is this place?"

"Who knows?"

JJ resisted an urge to scowl at his maker. The home's age was exactly the sort of thing Arek should have researched, but of course that would require work.

Arek snapped his fingers. "Sesh," he said.

"What?"

"Daniel *Sesh*."

"Repeating it doesn't make me understand, Arek."

"Think about it! An original, all-silver Lowrider Box installed ... what ... hundreds of years ago? In an old colonial home? And the owner's name is 'Sesh'? All the way back, *Seshes* probably owned this land."

"So?"

"Don't you get it?" Arek said, excited now. "'Sesh' *has* to be an abbreviated form of 'Bonesesh'! As in 'Donal of Bonesesh,' the necromancer!"

"You don't know that," JJ said. He sort of didn't *want* to know it. He was compelled by his maker bond to help Arek on his quest, but this was a quest JJ hoped they'd never finish.

"Come on," Arek replied. "*Silver vault?* Even if these

bumpkins could afford something like that, where would they get one? How would they install it?" He picked off more plaster. "Look. This brickwork is ancient, but the vault's still beneath it. This wasn't added later. It's been here all along. I thought we'd find a clue, but we found the goddamn finish line instead!"

"Well ..."

Arek wasn't interested in *well*. He was too excited. "This is incredible! Who would have thought the Demon's Keep would be in New Jersey?"

JJ thought that, but the jokes were too obvious.

Arek was scrambling, more eager than ever to find a way inside. "Help me get this mortar off. You can stop ramming it, at least. I guess that explains why you're a pussy."

"You're welcome," said JJ, but Arek didn't hear him. It *did* explain that. It also explained why he kept wanting to barf: all that silver just inches from his skin. Arek was reckless for not taking his discomfort seriously. What would have happened if the door over the silver had given way? He'd have smashed into it face-first and melted his face like taffy.

"*Immortality,*" Arek purred. "The very *idea* is intoxicating."

Yeah. For Arek. Personally, JJ had no interest in true immortality. He was close to immortal now, and it was a pain in the ass. What would it mean if he literally *couldn't die?* That sounded far worse than death. You'd live until the sun went supernova, survive the blast, then suffocate through empty space for all eternity. Being a God couldn't possibly be all it was cracked up to be.

"Look," JJ said. "I don't mean to dampen your enthusiasm, but how exactly do you plan to get two vampires into a vault made of silver?"

Arek, not listening, had removed enough brick to reveal a set of grooves in the silver. JJ, watching, then understood. The Keep was part of a bargain, according to legend. It had been made by human sorcerers, then kept by vampires. Both species were allowed access — because once inside, the silver dampened vampire abilities and made them almost human. Anything stored inside a Lowrider Box could therefore be kept safe while also remaining accessible. It was the only way both sides could win.

Arek bit his wrist, then dripped blood into the grooves of the lock. JJ, surprised Arek hadn't demanded *he* make the sacrifice, felt queasy just watching. He'd had no idea they were this close to a motherlode of silver, and seeing it now felt like skipping through Chernobyl. No lasting damage would be done unless he died here, but he still swore his insides were turning to mush.

Arek pulled his hand back. He had to take an extra step before his wound knitted, thanks to all the silver. They watched the grooved lock, waiting to see what would happen next.

The door opened like a bank vault. It was three inches thick with massive crude bolts. JJ would never have rammed his way through that — never in a million years. He'd told Arek as much: *It's a wooden door. If I can't just walk right through it, there's a reason.* But Arek never listened — not unless it was his own neck on the line.

The space behind wasn't a root cellar at all. Instead it was a cube-shaped room approximately twenty feet on each side: the size of a moderate garage. The surfaces were corroded and filthy, less like silver and more like the outside of a spent muffler. The walls were hung with a museum's worth of artifacts: all of them dark, all of them thick with necromantic history. The floor was laid with a walkway of planks so old, they looked like they might disintegrate when stepped on: the only way vampires could cross the silver.

Seeing it all made JJ look backward, toward the main part of the house where Elia Sesh watched her shows. The room obviously hadn't been sealed for radon. Did she know the Keep was here? JJ guessed not, but her son obviously had — and so had her husband, and his father, and *his* father. Tragic, that the last keeper was Daniel. Daniel struck JJ less as a legit sorcerer and more like a horrible actor who played one on TV. And not a very good station, either.

Arek was still gaping into the vault. At the end of the wooden walkway was a stone plinth. Atop the plinth was a book.

Arek put one foot on the walkway and began to move. It was more sound than it seemed. It moaned under Arek's feet, but did not falter. JJ followed — just halfway at first, then farther as Arek reached the book and began flipping pages.

"We're protecting it, JJ," he said. "If the Keepers' line is gone, *we* will become its custodians. This is God's work we're doing."

JJ frowned. He was pretty sure God knew Arek's name, but not in a good way.

Arek grinned as he found the page he'd been seeking most of JJ's vampire life. JJ had hoped the information on it was a rumor — this supposed *elixir of true immortality* — but no: Here the recipe was, right in front of them.

"It requires blood," Arek read.

Shocking. Everything in vampire lore seemed to require blood.

"Blood of the ancestor," Arek went on. "Incantation of the wise."

JJ came to read over Arek's shoulder. The text was

written in runes and had faded almost to nothing. The pages had clearly been turned on a regular basis — probably by Daniel, whose legacy struck JJ as "goth," not "guardian." It'd probably been more cool to him than real.

"It's totally faded," said JJ. "Look at this section here. You said 'ancestor,' but it almost looks like the rune for 'descendent.'"

"That's because at that time, the same rune was used for both concepts."

"So it's *'ancestor or descendent: pick one'*?" JJ shook his head. "It must be one or the other."

Arek didn't look from the page. "Our bloodlines were considered to be beyond time by the ancients. It doesn't matter which way you go. Up or down the family tree; it's all the same."

JJ sighed. "I guess that means you need *my* blood? *Again?*"

Arek was still translating. "It's talking about the *human* family tree, not the vampire tree. For the spell to work, you need genes passed down through human reproduction — from the life you had *before* you were turned vampire."

"That doesn't make any sense."

"Sure it does. A human necromancer wrote it. This tome was supposed to have a foot in both worlds, not just ours. It would be strange if it *didn't* tie back to the human world."

"But how the hell are you going to find human blood ... from someone in your *primary genetic line*?"

"I can either locate the blood of my parents, or their parents, or *their* parents ..."

"I see. So: blood drawn eighty or more years ago, from those specific people. Probably a lot of that just lying around."

"... *or the blood of my descendents. My human, chromosomal* descendents."

"We shoot blanks. It's not like you can have kids now."

Arek seemed annoyed. That wasn't technically the way things were. Vampire sperm was plentiful in number. It was just ... kind of undead. "From before I was made," he corrected.

"What are you talking about?"

Arek took the book from the plinth and walked past him, his expression deep in thought. He left JJ to close the door, then to follow.

"What the hell are you doing now?" JJ asked as he followed his maker through the house.

"I thought it might need ancestral blood," Arek answered, speaking more to himself now than JJ. "The old ones were so big on ancestral blood."

"And?"

Arek kept on walking. Through the living room, out the front door. JJ rushed after him, stopping to look Mrs. Sesh in the eyes and say, "You have no desire to dress like a Teletubby." Then he double-took, went back to her, and said, "But you are going to look into Meals on Wheels, and rethink the whole 'shut-in' thing."

"I am a party monster," the old woman replied.

JJ said, "Close enough."

Once outside, JJ took Arek by the shoulder and turned him around. They were in plain sight, spotlit by a street lamp. If anyone was watching, there'd only be a few interpretations: Either Old Lady Sesh had relatives the neighborhood hadn't seen before, she'd been robbed, or she'd finally started hiring gigolos.

"What's going on here, Arek? You act like you're not surprised."

"I'm not. I knew it'd be something like this. All I needed was the incantation, and now I've got it." He hefted the ancient book, careful not to jostle.

"*And* a living human relative. A *direct* relative. Not a cousin — someone in your direct bloodline. How are you going to manage that? I know you never had kids."

"As it turns out, I might have," Arek said. "I spent the night with a few women right before I was turned. I did some genealogy research a while back because I thought it might be like this." He held up his cell phone as if it was proof. "The internet says one of those women gave birth to a boy at just the right time."

"But ... even if that *is* your kid, by now, he might be—"

"—dead," Arek said, nodding. "And he is. But he had a kid. And then his kid had a kid."

"Then what?"

"Then Arcadia."

"Arcadia, Pennsylvania, or Arcadia, Texas?"

"Detroit," Arek answered.

"Detroit's a city, not a state," JJ said.

"Really?" Arek replied. "I've never been."

TWO

DETROIT

Orlo watched Amelie's head pop up. She'd streaked her bright red hair with purple for the tournament. The guild (including Amelie) couldn't decide if it was a good look or not, but in Orlo's personal opinion, Amelie couldn't really do anything wrong. If she buzzed all of that wonderful red hair off or pierced something dangly or got a face tattoo, Orlo would still find her intoxicating.

"Did someone say my name?" she asked.

"No," said Robert. He was polishing his armor, answering without paying attention. Orlo figured this game wouldn't require armor, but he was already regretting his presumption. *Neck* armor? Of course that'd come in handy. Protection at the neck, in fact, might turn out to be essential.

"I just heard someone yell 'Amelie,'" Amelie said.

"I think they said 'Arcadia,'" Nora replied.

"I'd better go check." Amelie rose and walked to the Game Master table. Orlo watched her go until he saw Nora looking at him. Then he went back to filling out his character sheet.

"Where are you guys writing down your weapons?" asked Jaden.

Orlo had been wondering the same thing. Information on the tournament had been bare-bones. The organizers knew how viciously the competitors would fight for the prize and hence seemed to be wary of cheating. Less information ahead of time meant less chance to exploit loopholes. That wouldn't be necessary for a punching tournament, Orlo had said earlier, because the people who entered that tournament would be too dumb to cheat — unlike this enormous think tank of nerds and geeks.

Everyone looked to Nora. Nora was pens and paper, Excel and databases. She knew every point her character had ever earned and what for, all the way back to the first limb her character lost in the battle of Durmont versus Talluria, in which she'd been an elf or something. Orlo couldn't remember. Personally, he had three or four characters going and used them willy-nilly. Today's was a modified version of his most common character: Shadow Stalker, a vigilante merchant in their usual fantasy world and a disillusioned cop turned vampire hunter in this one. The idea of dragging a middle-ages character to the Detroit Marlowe Center for a game set in present day was a bit anachronistic, but Orlo solved it by doffing Shadow Stalker's usual robe and trading it for a trenchcoat.

"What?" Nora asked.

"What should we do for weapons?" Jaden asked. Jaden was so typical and ordinary that you could lose him in a large room. He was maybe five-eight, fluffy light-colored hair, and could have been the prototype for the modern dork. It was hard not to love him because even in play, Jaden tended to believe. When they battled in D&D, Jaden was thinking of all those real dragons out there, hiding in caves. When wizards cast spells, Jaden researched the spells as if they were real, convinced that game magic had its roots in actual magic. Had to, right? All legends came from somewhere.

"How should I know?" Nora asked.

"Because you always know."

"But I *don't* know."

"Except that you do, right?" Jaden raised his eyebrows, playing with her. Nora sighed and opened the small player manual the organizers had given each team and began flipping pages.

Amelie returned. "I heard wrong," she announced. "They said 'Arcadia.'"

"Who did?"

"I don't know," she said. Clearly she'd asked someone, but apparently it was too much to say who. Good thing it didn't matter.

"Oh, and Jason Guerey says hi."

Brody, who'd been off in his own world, looked up. Brody was 25 and might just be the nicest guy Orlo had ever met. He was also the most mainstream-looking of the men in the guild — enough that he got looks from women, even while he was in costume, that weren't full of pity.

"No," he said. "*Guerey's* here?"

Amelie nodded. "Yeah. I saw him over by the snack machines." She pointed, and all six of the others looked. And yes, there Guerey was, pulling on a long black coat and a bandolier strung with six-inch wooden garden stakes.

Brody sat back down. "I thought his guild kicked him out?"

"Apparently not," said Amelie. "I saw a few of the others over there, too. Who I *didn't* see was Marta and Greg. I'm guessing that instead of kicking Jason out, they pulled a mutiny or something. They got rid of guild leadership instead."

"So who's leading them?"

"Dunno. Jason, probably. I didn't stop to chat. We'll have to deal with them enough during the game."

Orlo was still looking up. She'd been standing for too long.

"Aren't you going to sit?" he asked.

"Well, that's the thing," she said. "I figured adding a corset would be a good idea, but it sort of locked up while I was walking around just now."

"So you can't sit?"

"Can't sit, can't bend. But maybe that's okay? Tell me it is. Because look how pretty!"

She extended her arms to show off her wardrobe. She'd made it herself just like all her game costumes, and like all the others in her guild, her outfit didn't really match any particular time or place. Her character was Lady Elizabeth Jane Warwick, a descendent of the Noble House of Beaumont stretching back to Hong Kong during the Opium War. That didn't particularly make sense for the scenario, but it made at least as much sense as Robert AKA Mack Knight, who wore an Army Ranger uniform with a foam sword or Brody AKA Virgo Blackheart, who looked like one of the Knights Templar. Anything went in this hodgepodge.

"Beautiful," said Nora. "But as this guild's strategy planner ..."

Amelie made an annoyed face, said, "Oh, fine, whatever, I'll be practical if I have to," and began removing the corset. Watching gave Orlo a boner, so he looked away.

"*Nora.* Where are we on the weapons question?" Jaden asked.

Amelie looked over with her corset halfway off. "What weapons question?"

"It took me forever to win my plus-three mace," said Rohit. "Bitches *better* let me use my plus-three mace."

"Here it is," said Nora, flattening the player manual. "'No external weapons will be allowed. All weapons are provided in-game.'"

"What the shizzle?" said Rohit. "That ain't cool."

"No weapons?" That was Robert, with his hand on his sword. He'd made it for a fantasy event two weeks ago but hadn't been able to use it because he'd left the hilt exposed, and there was no time to modify it for re-approval in time. He'd been talking for the entire ride up about how excited he was to finally have a real blade of his own.

"That's what it says," Nora told him. "We'll all start with a small balance and can earn more as we play. We have to either find or buy weapons from sellers in-game." She closed the manual. "Must be another way they're trying to level the playing field."

"That's bullshit," said Robert. Robert was about as broad as a lamppost and had hair like a 1920s Vaudeville performer. All he needed was a cane and he could be Charlie Chaplin. "I've worked forever to build up enough experience to—"

"New game, new rules. But hey. At least everyone's on the same footing." Nora pointed toward where they'd seen their rivals. "They always beat us because they enter more events and rack up more experience. We're always saying it's not fair: If *we* had time and money to enter that many events, we'd have a ton of points, too." Nora raised her bare, waif-thin arms and waved them about the convention center, making her short brunette bob shake like an animal on her head. "Now those points don't matter. Now *every-*

one's at zero. We got what we wanted. Let's not bitch too much about it."

"Doesn't that make you nervous," asked Brody, "not knowing what to obsess over?"

Nora gave him an annoyed, *nyah-nyah* look that was half tongue, half rolled eyes. Brody chuckled.

The loudspeaker crackled. As all eyes lifted from preparation and registration, the lights went almost entirely out, then back on, then off and on again. The windows were blocked so that real-world time wouldn't intrude while the game was on, so between clicks, the darkness was nearly complete.

A commotion began. A line of intense-looking people advanced through three contiguous sets of double doors leading into the central theater, all dressed in gothic red and black. Lots of leather. Lots of eye makeup and bone-white foundation. Even from here, Orlo could see their fake teeth sparkle.

Only Brody hadn't looked up after mocking Nora. Rohit elbowed him.

"What?"

"Check it out," Rohit told him. "The vampires are here."

THREE
LARP

Nora Qualley, age 22 and recent Stanford dropout, was, in her own opinion, kind of a mess. To everyone else (other than her parents, naturally), the exact opposite was true. For every organizational, got-her-shit-together shortcoming Nora saw in herself, the most competent members of her guild had things three times as bad. Before she'd joined them, they had no plan at all. They'd been four boys then (Brody, Rohit, Orlo, and a kid named Gerard who had breath so bad they'd kicked him out and said it was for personal reasons), and at first they'd balked at the idea of adding estrogen to their mix. They gave her a chance at Orlo's insistence and immediately their game improved tenfold. For Nora, the improvements were beyond obvious: the equivalent of remembering to put wheels on the car before driving it. For the boys, though, Nora's tweaks were a revelation. Nora decided not to rock the boat. She let them think of her obvious steps as miracle work, and she'd been with them ever since.

Despite praise from the boys (and Amelie for the past two years; she always forgot about Amelie), Nora always felt she was doing something wrong. Not *everything*; Nora wasn't so deluded as to feel she did nothing right. But *something*. Always *something*. When she couldn't pinpoint the *something* she was doing wrong, she became nervous, sure that the Devil you knew was always better than the Devil you couldn't see. She knew that Devil had to be there, though, because there was *always* a flaw. *Always* a shortcoming. If Nora couldn't see the shortcoming, that was bad news. It'd trip her when she least expected it.

So she never rested. Never stopped looking for what might go wrong.

Before college, her Devil was a lack of ambition — or so Mom and Dad told her. She was near the top of her high school class, a superb track athlete who nearly merited a scholarship, and treasurer of Student Council at a school where Student Council actually meant something. Still, she didn't apply for colleges as early as she'd planned — and once she started applying, her parents pointed out that she wasn't putting enough effort into each of her essays. She didn't repeat essays, either: OSU's application asked for her greatest achievement and U of M's application asked for her greatest achievement, but rather than sending the same essay to both schools, she wrote two. Still, by her parental standards, her diligence was lackluster — and so by Nora's standards, her diligence was lackluster, too.

She got into every college she applied to, but was offered a scholarship by only four of the six. Mom said it was because she hadn't applied herself. She settled for Stanford on a fifty percent ride, took every honors course she could her freshman year, then burned out and was sent home with nervous exhaustion. She began therapy over her mother's protests, but the therapist turned out to be a subversive scoundrel. He encouraged Nora to do *less*, not more. He encouraged her to *take it easy*, not work harder. Nora, if not for the guilt, would have liked his advice just fine.

It was hard to be Nora Qualley. It was so much easier to be her character, Camille Usher. Camille, like Nora, was a student — but unlike Nora, Camille had graduated college, begun a graduate degree in anthropology, and generally gotten her shit together. Nora had ambitions in anthropology as well, but for now "finding herself" (Dr. White's words) was more important than school. So while Nora worked a job in retail to her parents' dismay, she spent break and lunch hours fleshing out her live action role-play ("LARP") character, making Camille more real than even Nora.

At first it was odd, maybe a little embarrassing. She'd seen people doing LARP in the park, battling foam swords against cardboard armor. It struck Nora as pathetic and sad. Now, that same "pathetic" hobby didn't seem pathetic at all. Instead, it was empowering. It was, for stressed-out Nora, a lifesaver. Her parents didn't know she LARPed, and whenever someone accidentally mentioned "Camille Usher" around them, Nora pretended Camille was a friend rather than her alter-ego. Meanwhile she totaled Camille's points and aligned her talents with her missions, always setting her duties in the guild to maximize what Camille could do. Ironically, she was optimizing better now than she had as a student. Ironically, she was a better real-life anthropologist now than she'd have been if she'd toughed it out at Stanford.

This long weekend's LARP would be a new trial for Nora and Camille. Every player had to start from zero in terms of experience, weapons, and armor. Every player, however, could submit any character and attribute set they wished as long as that character was a vampire hunter, a civilian, a cop, or a detective — basically anything other than a vampire. There was a loophole, though — and true to Nora, she'd already found and exploited it. Like the movie vampire hunter Blade, Camille's backstory included a vampire attack, then a partial-vampire resurrection. Camille, like Blade, was a daywalker. It was a new twist and one Nora planned to keep for Camille in any games that allowed it. And why not? Their normal swords-and-shields LARPs took place in the fantasy world of Elah, and Elah's lore included wizards and sorcerers — so why not half-vampires? It was still magic, not too different from the necromancer Brody sometimes played.

The allowances she'd argued from the Game Master over the past weeks included:

1. Camille could glamour humans, but it was more like persuasion than must-obey commands.

2. She could get a sense of what nearby vampires were thinking, but only if they were planning something big ... and only at the expense of experience points she'd yet to accumulate.

3. She had more strength than humans, and once she got her hands on a weapon, that weapon would inflict 1.5x damage.

But those advantages didn't come cheap. In exchange, Camille had weaknesses the humans didn't: She'd need to drink an herbal concoction every two game-hours, and if she couldn't find any of it (or the herbs to brew it), her strength for the next two hours would be diminished by half. She'd be weaker in the game's designated daylight hours as well, though she could minimize that weakness by applying a kind of magical sunscreen, which she'd need to find and buy in-game. All were trades Nora was willing to make. She was plenty wily enough to manage all the details. LARP, unlike college, was something she'd been born for. It was a hobby she excelled at without strain or stress.

When the vampires emerged from the central theater, Nora watched them with hard eyes. She pretended they were real vampires, trying to sink into character. It wasn't easy; the organizers had brought them out for orientation, not to begin the game. The fact that she hadn't yet donned her pseudo-Victorian garb and was still copying Nora's driver's license number onto a liability waiver broke the illusion a bit.

Nora tried anyway. The tournament took place in the modern age, but vampires (and often vampire hunters) didn't conform precisely to calendar time. For that reason, although it was hard to imagine Camille Usher having a driver's license, she could definitely have one. With her high-collared dresses and tall black boots, Camille was more the type to hire a horse coach, riding up to Joe Lewis Arena over foggy Scottish moors.

A tall woman with short blonde hair moved in front of the vampires, holding a microphone.

"Hello and welcome to Vampire Dominion, the Great Lakes Fantasy Association's first-ever multi-day LARP event!" she said, her voice augmented by microphone and speakers. "My name is Lissa Whitman. I'm this event's organizer, but I'll also be your head referee for the weekend." She smiled wide. "I'll be honest; we didn't know how popular an event like this would be. It was kind of a gut check to rent this entire building for three full days! I was just hoping we could cover our butts, but the community here has been great and we did a lot more than just cover butts. So thank you. We love role-playing games as much as you do, and our goal all along has just been to have some fun."

There was light applause. Some chatter.

"How many of you have LARPed before?"

Only half of the hands went up. That was surprising; Nora didn't think so many newbies would commit to such a large first event. But then again, LARPers, including herself, tended to be more confident in character than out of character. It was possible a lot of should-be-raised hands were shy.

"Great. Keep those hands up," said Lissa Whitman. "Now look around at the people near you whose hands *aren't* up. Remember your first event? Kind of overwhelming, right? You probably had no idea what to do, where to go, or what the rules really were even if someone explained them. My first game, I got into a fight. It was a fantasy event and I thought leather armor gave me two extra strikes when it really only gave me one. I didn't go down after being hit because I was confused, and someone took issue with it. If anything like that happens here, try to remember that half of you have never done this before. Be cool about it, and talk first instead of assuming the other person is trying to get away with something. This is an inclusive organization. Hell, this is an inclusive *activity*. Let's not be like the cool kids in school, okay? So Rule Number One?" She held a finger high. "Don't be an asshole."

"I like her already," said Amelie.

"Rule Number Two is more of a guideline: Forget rules from other events you've attended. We've reinvented the wheel and only a few things matter at the start. Most obviously, it's your team versus the other teams — and all teams, of course, ultimately battle our vampires." She gestured to the goth-looking men and women behind her in dramatic makeup and leather. "In the event of a melee, standard battle rules apply: If you're hit in a limb, you have to tuck that limb back and can't use it. If you're struck in the torso or head, that's a mortal wound, subject to any armor you're wearing. Once you're dead, lay down unless you're getting stepped on. You can re-spawn most times, but not all; there are a few places you'll see where those who die are out for good unless they want to re-enter as an NPC to finish out the weekend. Re-spawn time in Vampire Dominion, unless a ref tells you otherwise, is fifteen minutes. Assuming the battle that killed you is over by then, you can get back up and keep playing."

Whitman paced, shifting eye contact to keep the group's attention.

"But you won't see big battles like that often in this game. It's just not designed that way. Those of you who've LARPed before — which of you have done *vampire* LARP?"

Maybe ten percent of the people in the room raised their hands.

"The Vampire Dominion experience is as visceral as you want it to be, and it will span the entire floor. Our vampire volunteers have been instructed to organize in small covens, not huge encampments. The reason is because with so many teams in play, we can't have everyone going to the same people and following the same exact paths. So *spread out.* Everyone you encounter in the game will have something to tell you, making this more like a dinner theater mystery than a blood-soaked horror show. But hey, opportunities do still abound. This is a three-day, three-floor event with over two hundred participants and nearly as many volunteers, and the sheer size of it means there's something for everyone. If you want to get into a blood orgy, knock yourself out."

Whitman waved her hands as if to reset.

"I'm getting ahead of myself. Probably confusing some

of you. When I asked if any of you have done Vampire LARP before, the point was to demonstrate that ... what? ... eighty-ninety percent of you are new to this style and genre. If you've LARPed at all, you've probably heard over and over, 'No two LARP events are the same.' Well, that's even truer here." She held out one hand and ticked off points on her fingers as she continued. "This isn't like a White Wolf game, it's not like a Texas Splatterpunk style game, and it's not an existing game that you're joining using an existing character and experience. As I'm sure the Game Master table already told you, everyone here is starting fresh. Nobody has any idea of the game's trajectory and nobody has built status for themselves. If you're an innkeeper, good for you. You *just* opened your inn and you don't have any regulars. You haven't learned that vampires come in all the time, and hence wear armor and have a shotgun full of silver buckshot under the counter. Or, if you're a vampire hunter like most of you, keep in mind that you haven't explored the world and found any powerful artifacts before game-start. You don't know the rules of our world's vampires. All of that, you get to figure out as you go."

Brody raised his hand.

"Yes?"

Heads turned toward Brody. Nora saw Jason Guerey's team look in Brody's direction as well. A look of recognition crossed many faces. Eyebrows lowered. There was professional courtesy there, but some bad feelings, too.

"Are the vampires in this game ... like ... *Anne Rice* vampires?"

Whitman smiled. "I guess you'll have to figure that out."

"Sunlight kills them, though, right?"

"Yes. I'll give you that one."

"What about crosses? Holy water? Can they walk on sacred ground?"

Whitman chuckled. "All things you'll have to learn by doing. I will say, though, that our vampires don't sparkle."

The whole room laughed, Nora included. She'd actually read *Twilight* and enjoyed it, and she knew Jaden had read it as well — more for research in Jaden's case.

"One thing we *did* take from Anne Rice vampires," Whitman continued, "is their carnal nature. Maybe this is a little un-PC, but here goes: Our vampires are DTF."

"'DTF'?" Amelie asked her group, keeping her voice low.

"'Down to fuck,'" Rohit explained with a lecherous wink.

"We considered softening that aspect of things," Whitman explained, "but it just felt ... *wrong* somehow. Vampires live in covens, and the act of feeding is sensual by nature. A lot of early survey data we got — all of it confidential — was that, frankly, a lot of players especially like the idea of getting out of their everyday skins and being people they can't be day to day ... including in that way."

"That means everyone wants an excuse to get up on each other, then blame the game for turning them into sex maniacs," Rohit said. "Perverts, all of us."

"Still," Whitman went on, "we realize that's not for all of you. Some folks are shy, some are maybe a little more asexual than others, and some just don't like the idea of having strangers all over their neck as part of a turning ceremony. If that's you, you can opt out. All you have to do is say the name of the game: 'Vampire Dominion.' Say that and the sexy stuff stops, and you'll just be declared turned, or whatever the case may be."

"Like a safeword when you're tied up and someone's whipping you, and you can't take it anymore," said Rohit.

"Grow up, Rohit," said Orlo. He was saying it for Nora and Amelie's benefit, which was both sweet and unnecessary; both were big girls who could take care of themselves.

Whitman pointed to a group of people wearing Day-Glo orange armbands. "The only other thing you really need to know before I let you finish your paperwork is 'safety and common decency first.' Obey your officials—" Another wave to the armband crew. "—and just be cool, decent people to one another. If you're in a fight, don't prove how amazing you are by hitting them harder than you have to. The in-game weapons are foam and won't hurt anyone, but still try to use common sense. If you use our 'silver' restraints, don't tighten them too far and back off if someone says 'Vampire Dominion.' If you're using a chain weapon, like a morning star, always swing in short arcs over the top—" She demonstrated with a downward swing. "—rather than from the side, where you might get someone's neck. If someone yells 'HOLD,' freeze right where you are and repeat 'HOLD' until everyone's frozen. Freeze *right* where you are, meaning that if you're in the middle of a step, don't put your foot down, or do so very, *very* carefully. A lot of holds happen because something's dropped, and we don't want you stepping on it. Everyone understand?"

The room nodded.

"All right, then," she said, smiling wider. "Remember. All of our vampires are NPCs. If you run into a vampire, that's not a player, that's a volunteer. It means they know the rules better than you do. If you think vampirism should work one way and they say otherwise, they're right and you're wrong. This isn't a battle royale game. It's quieter, and investigative. You'll get a short brief at the opening bell, but for now what's in the player guide and what I just told you is all you need to know." She stood tall and clapped her hands over her head. "Okay! I show ..." She looked at her watch. "... exactly 33 minutes left until 10am. Are you ready?"

The room cheered.

"Then finish up ... and let's get our blood on!"

FOUR
FLYING SPAGHETTI MONSTER

Inside Robert's imagination, his character Mack Knight looked a little like a real-life GI Joe and a little like the comic superhero Kick-Ass. The rules of Vampire Dominion forbade it, but often Mack wore two batons on his back and wielded them in a decidedly Kick-Ass way. He'd need a different strategy this weekend, hunting these vampires.

Mack was — of course — a kick-ass kind of guy. At medieval and fantasy events, Mack was called "Michael" and wore robes instead of an Army uniform, but to Robert, his usual character and the modified version he'd wear today were basically the same. Mack, like Michael, had a rich backstory. Both men (since they were the *same* man) had once been priests. Mack would soon fight vampires, yes ... but mostly Robert's characters fought for the glory of God against whichever infidel the game required. Mack, like real-life Robert, prayed nightly. Mack always asked forgiveness for the lives he'd ended. It wasn't all kick-ass. There was piety and penance in there, too.

Robert attended his first LARP event after Rohit basically forced him. Rohit and Robert were unlikely friends: Rohit outgoing and popular in his own way, Robert sometimes too shy to order food at a drive-thru. Rohit seemed to feel it was his duty to drag Robert out of his shell — so Robert, knowing this about himself, attended despite overwhelming nerves. Robert thought he might be borderline autistic (he'd never been tested) and worried the game's intensity and noise might send him spiraling. The opposite turned out to be true. He was shy at first, but warmed up quickly. Once in costume, Robert found himself able to be all the things he'd never been. It was easy. Completely effortless.

After the event was over, Robert wanted more. And more. Soon LARPing (at events around once a month, in the park most other weekends) was all he wanted to do. It kept him from having to be his closed-in self. It made him larger than life.

But Robert's mother and father didn't, at first, agree. The games Rohit played were thick with lore and fantasy, including such unmentionables as wizards and dark creatures, of which Robert's devout Christian folks disapproved. He'd tried vampire LARP before as well, telling his parents that he and Rohit were just going camping. If Mom and Dad disapproved of normal LARP's unholy elements, what would they think of Godless creatures who sucked blood and retreated from crosses and holy water? To soothe their objections, Robert emphasized Mack/Michael's Crusader aspects. He told them he wasn't merely *playing*; he was teaching heathen youth the glory of God through Mack/Michael's teachings. Most times, though, he just lied. His parents were absentee enough not to ask twice. This weekend, for instance, Robert was officially attending an

Academic Decathlon event, not LARPing. Good thing his parents were too busy with work to know Robert wasn't on the AD team and never had been.

Now Robert was polishing Mack's enormous gold cross, which he always wore beneath his Ranger uniform to keep the power of God close to his heart. Rohit picked it up. Robert tried to snatch it back, but Rohit held it far like a game of Keep Away.

"Hey, what the crap?" Robert said.

Rohit shrugged. "They said no powers. No props."

"That's just part of Mack's costume!"

"No, it's how he repels the Flying Spaghetti Monster. What will happen if we meet the Flying Spaghetti Monster in this game? You'll have an unfair advantage."

Robert snatched again. Rohit held the cross farther while Robert grasped his torso.

"Hey!" Rohit shouted to a passing official. "Are we allowed to use Voodoo? We're not, right?" Then to Robert, even though the official had ignored him: "Told you."

Rohit let Robert take the cross, which he did with aggression.

"You're an asshole."

Rohit was unfazed. "You do this to get away from all your parents' shit. Why do you need a damn cross?"

"It's not mine. It's Mack's."

"Fine," Rohit said. "Why does *Mack* need it?"

"It's part of his faith."

"Definitely not part of Mom and Dad's faith?"

"Let it go, Rohit."

"Remember the time I was over for dinner, and your mom asked if I believed in God, and I asked which one?"

Yes. That had been uncomfortable. It was a laugh for

Rohit, but a pain in the ass for Robert. Rohit could do drive-by witticisms in the name of fun, but Robert had to live with the consequences. Every time thereafter when Robert went out, he was questioned: *Is that brown boy going? Where are his parents?* The second question always seemed rhetorical to Robert. Mom really seemed to be asking if Rohit's folks were at their coven meeting, sacrificing virgins or whatever Indians did.

Robert straightened his uniform collar, then put the cross over his head and tucked it beneath his shirt. He kept a wary eye on Rohit the entire time, half challenge and half expectation that he'd say or do something stupid. But Rohit just let it happen with a full-body sigh, then let the issue go.

"I've been looking at the guide," Rohit said, settling back in a make-peace way. "Unless they give us a lot more when the game begins, we've kind of got dick to work with. I guess we have to work it all out for ourselves. So what I'm thinking is, we split up. Take separate missions."

"Why?"

"So we'll learn stuff faster."

"But we'll be more vulnerable," Robert countered. "You know the hunter clans are allowed to war with each other, and the vampires can turn them into sleeper agents if they get the chance?"

Rohit shrugged. "Acceptable risk. There's so much ground to cover, in terms of what we need to figure out about the vampires — where they are, how to kill them, what artifacts we need, shit like that — but also literally. This place is enormous."

"We only have to worry about the first floor on Day One," Robert said.

"It's still enormous. Even taking out the cafeteria safe zone, it's a ton of ground. And from this?" He shook the player guide. "I get the feeling they're using it all. Like every nook and cranny. I wouldn't be surprised if they hid clues in the vents."

"I'm sure we won't have to go into the vents."

"Could make for some cool secret passageways, though," said Rohit. "Stay away from the spies and other teams."

"I'm sure we're not *supposed* to go into the vents," Robert clarified.

Amelie came over and sat beside them.

"Uh-oh," said Rohit. "It's the missus."

Amelie ignored him. "I was talking to Shadow Stalker."

"Do we really have to use in-game names before the clock starts?"

"Yes," said Robert and Amelie together. Then Robert added, "It just helps me get into character."

"Okay. But then you have to deal with my accent. Vitch es like dis, *einverstanden?*"

"Fine," Amelie said, giving up. "I was talking to *Orlo*, then." Everyone hated the accent Rohit had developed for his character Baron Helmut von Baden, which Robert secretly suspected was the reason Rohit insisted upon it. It was like language warfare. When he wanted to remain out-of-game (like now) or when he wanted to win an in-game argument, he laid Helmut's accent on particularly thick. Usually the other party surrendered just so they wouldn't have to hear it anymore.

"Anyway, Orlo was talking to this girl ..."

"Was her name Nora?"

"No, it was Hippolyta."

Rohit made a face. "Ugh. Unfortunate name."

"More unfortunate than 'Baron Helmut von Baden'?"

"Hey, 'Helmut' is a seriously badass—"

Robert cut Rohit off. "Why do I know that name?"

"Amazon warrior queen? You know, like Wonder Woman?"

They both looked at Rohit, paused, then back at each other.

"She's in Jason's guild," Amelie explained. "She's actually the new guild leader."

"Are we really *guilds*, if we're vampire hunters today?" Rohit asked.

"Why wouldn't we be?"

Rohit shrugged. "Dunno. I mean: *vampire hunters*. That's a different kind of awesome than usual. I'd think they'd be in organizations. Or leagues. Remember that one league? The one with all the extraordinary gentlemen in it?"

"Shut up, Rohit," said Amelie. Then to Robert: "Where was I?"

"Orlo, Hippo girl ..."

"Oh, right. She said she asked the Game Master about the mission objectives for each day. And the Game Master said—"

"She can't ask about that yet!"

Amelie held up a hand to Rohit, saying both, *Let me finish* and *If you don't stop interrupting me, I will hurt you.* She could do it easily. She'd grown up with seven older brothers, six of whom were now weekend MMA fighters, following in the footsteps of Dad, a former boxer. Robert, like Orlo, kept hoping they'd end up in a fight so she'd could maim some fuckers.

"She wasn't asking what the objectives *were*," Amelie continued. "She was asking if we'd *find out* what they were at the opening bell, or if we'd have to work them out during the game. The GM said it was the latter, but their guild's theory is that scoring has more to do with with placement for the following day than getting a relic or anything like that. Because if it's a relic, we'd all have to get it and there's like a million teams here."

"How would that work?" Robert asked.

"Like pool play before a sports tournament, where how well you do in pool play determines where you start in the tournament bracket. For us, scoring well today might mean a head start tomorrow. Or more supplies than the next team down ... something like that."

"Who cares?" said Rohit. "Obviously we're going to do our best either way."

Amelie met his eyes. "I'm just telling you what I know. I also assume the overall objective will be to kill the vampire leader or something, but we probably won't get sight of that until tomorrow. At least."

They all nodded. It wasn't really new information, but it helped calibrate their expectations. This was the largest and longest LARP event anyone in the guild had ever done — probably *why* the organizers kept repeating how unique it was relative to other events. They were looking at three back-to-back seven-hour days with only a one-hour lunch break in the middle of each. Each night they'd get to regroup and review what they'd learned (Nora's favorite part; she'd never had a chance to analyze mid-event before), then head back out for new instructions in the morning. Six working hours times three days was eighteen hours total: a full waking day, basically. It was a lot of LARPing even for Robert's taste, but the prize was worth it: not just five thousand dollars to split, but also significant experience points for all of their characters should they choose to attend another Dominion event.

The lights flickered on and off. Then all three stood,

nodded to each other, nodded to the rest of their guild twenty feet away on the patterned carpet, and began a final once-over of their costumes.

It was 9:55am Eastern Standard Time, and Vampire Dominion was about to begin.

FIVE
DEAD AGAIN

11:04am by Brody's watch.

They were in a dark room made to look like a night-club, but according to the official game clock, it wasn't 11:04am; it was almost exactly 4:15am. The game clock for each day began at midnight, ran four times as fast as normal, and ended at game-midnight the next day — 5pm on the real-world clock. The design meant the "day" began with a few hours of in-game darkness and ended with a few more hours of in-game darkness, essentially bookending the game day with "vampire time," broken by "daytime" in the middle. The organizers had gone all-out, blocking the real windows with dark cloth and placing high-Kelvin "windows" along interior walls to simulate the progression from sunrise to sunset. Each room on the floor was set up to look not like one room among many, but its own structure with outside walls. There were sections of hallway made to look like they were outside, with those clever daylights overhead. It wasn't amazing production value in Brody's mind, but it was at least as good as the plays he'd been in — and overall excellent considering how much square footage they'd had to cover. Certainly the most elaborate LARP he'd ever been part of.

The nightclub, at 4am, was closed. After last call, even vampires had no interest in sticking around.

"There's nobody here," said Orlo. "I'm telling you, we should have gone into the ancient catacombs like everyone else."

Brody was in the lead. The guild, unlike most, was egalitarian. Orlo was nominally their leader, but in truth each of them had specialities and strengths. After two full years of LARPing together (and a year before that for Rohit, Orlo, and Brody), the guild had learned to work together like a well-oiled machine. Brody was best at starts. Amelie was often great at finishes. Logic puzzles deferred to Orlo or Rohit, Jaden was best at negotiations and rapport-building with allies, Robert handled lore, and Nora was the umbrella over all of them, tracking abilities, inventories, archives, and mundane-to-others details like game-clock management.

So Orlo, although he gave his opinion, didn't push when nobody murmured agreement. Brody's judgment would stand until circumstances or consensus for another course of action changed it.

"The fact that like two-thirds of the guilds went to the catacombs is *why* we shouldn't go there," Brody said. "Come on. It's an obvious decoy. *Catacombs?* In a *modern-setting* vampire game? It's a total cliche. The sun won't rise until ... what? 7am?"

Nora nodded, clarifying: "7:04." The game used the current real-world sunset and sunrise times so players who looked them up in advance could bank on them, which of course Nora already had.

"Still dark out," Brody said. "That means they'll be

somewhere else. Vampires aren't homebodies. Even if they're sleeping in the catacombs during daylight hours ..."

"Which they're not," said Rohit. "Again, too obvious."

Orlo nodded. That much, at least, Brody agreed with. The worst thing the vampires could do, especially so early in the game, would be to reveal their nesting places. All of the game's Van Helsings would just camp out, waiting for them to return with stakes sharpened. It would be death for the tournament if that happened, so there was no way the GMs would let it.

"Even if they're at the catacombs *sometimes*," Brody said, "they'll be out at *nighttime*. The GM wants us to interact with them, not spend all our time searching for nests that must, by definition, be extremely well-hidden."

"They might not even have nests," said Jaden.

"You guys mind?" Amelie said. "I'm trying to stay in-game here, but it's hard with everyone talking about 'Game Masters' and out-of-game logic."

Brody nodded. The slip had probably been his fault. The reason he was so good at beginnings was specifically due to the complaint Amelie had just lodged: Specifically, he didn't think *in-game* at all at the start. Instead, he tried to get inside the heads of the real-world organizers, considering the practical concerns they must have had in setting things up. It was like cheating in spirit (seeing as they were meant to spend in-game time *fully in-game* and in-character), but it wasn't technically cheating. Fair game, in other words.

But she was still right. They weren't supposed to be Brody and Orlo and Amelie right now. They were supposed to be playing their characters, and addressing each other as such.

"I'm sorry, Lady Elizabeth," Brody said, pitching his

voice to Virgo Blackheart's inflection. Virgo was more grandiose than Brody was, probably owing to his Templar lineage. "I felt it was worth the investigation."

"Why?" asked Nora. Or, technically: Camille Usher.

"Because strip clubs are full of debauchery. We know we are facing *saucy* beasts, right?"

Mumbling followed. Apparently the others didn't agree.

They made a circuit. The entire set was abandoned. It didn't look particularly used, either, which told Brody that it wasn't *abandoned* so much as *not in use yet*. In game time, there'd be two hours between game-start and last call — three hours, probably, until the club shut for the night. But in real time, that meant 30-45 minutes. Probably wasn't worth spinning up the set until game-evening, which wouldn't happen until sunset around 4 1/2 real-world hours from now.

They finished their survey. Brody/Virgo swept his robes behind him, his hand missing the comforting presence of his legendary silver vampire-killing blade ... which, because they were using in-game logic, "Virgo" assumed must have been lost instead of confiscated. "I still say it was worth a check. We know we're looking for witnesses to the murders last night, or to someone who was involved. It's as logical that they would be here as anywhere else."

"De murder vuz across town," said Rohit, AKA Helmut.

"Yes. But there was sawdust caked into the victim's boots," said Brody/Virgo. "The mill is west."

The others must have forgotten that, because they mumbled again and looked around with new eyes.

Nora, using her Camille Usher voice and wearing her customary small round sunglasses over her powdered face, said, "Maybe the convenience store, then? It's open 24 hours." She turned to Jaden, who wore a long black trench-coat with a textured black vest underneath. "Kaspar," she said to him. "When you spoke earlier with the man in the alley, did you get the feeling he—"

Something rustled. It was like the rapid-flutter wings of a very large bat. The group stopped, looked to where the sound seemed to have come from, then looked at each other. Robert put a finger to his lips and made military finger gestures that Brody thought were probably wrong but still got the message across: *Quiet. You two go that way, slowly. You two, opposite side. Everyone else take the middle. Stakes out.*

The only weapon they'd been allowed so far were simple wooden stakes. If their characters didn't already have blunted stakes with soft foam tips (many did), the organizers had provided a pile that was basically infinite. Handheld stakes weren't much use; you couldn't usually drive one all the way into the heart without a hammer, and good luck getting a vampire to hold still long enough for you to do it. The only one of them who had a real chance was Camille/Nora, with her daywalker blood. Until sunrise, she'd be almost as fast and strong as the vampires, though with her own disadvantages.

They did as Robert/Mack instructed, flanking a perhaps five-by-five cubicle along one wall that looked like an overly large confessional. It was probably a sex booth of some kind, ostensibly for private lap dances. All Brody knew — and this, again, he knew using that forbidden real-world logic — was that the chamber wasn't part of the usual conference center decor. The organizers would only have added if they meant to use it.

Robert/Mack held up a hand with five fingers extended. He lowered them one at a time for a countdown: *Five ... four*

... three ... two ... one. Watching and waiting, Brody felt his heart beat faster. That was the thing about LARP: It was nearly impossible to get hurt, but still each encounter had a way of feeling like life or death — especially in a quiet game like this where jump-scares were likely to be the norm.

Robert yanked the door while the others stood back. It wasn't fully open before the entire structure, designed as a break-apart, was kicked to pieces from the inside. The illusion was impressive; it was almost like a real undead creature had actually demolished it.

Two vampires rushed right at the forward group. Their mouths were open, fangs visible. The fangs were stained red, as were their lips. Brody/Virgo saw why even in all the confusion: On a still-intact wooden seat inside the enclosure, a human woman sprawled back with her neck bent and bleeding. Blood was everywhere.

The vampires moved as quickly as they were able, but one corner-of-the-eye look told Brody that officials had emerged from hiding places to watch, meaning they needed to do as they'd been told — to slow down to about half-speed themselves so the vampires would have a speed advantage. If vampires were real (Jaden, no shit, thought they might be), humans could never catch them, so the game was designed to give the volunteers the same advantage. *Walk like you're pushing your way through tar,* was the official instruction whenever vampires charged. Brody, along with all the others, was doing that now.

Nora/Camille was the exception — and a damn good thing, because the vampires they'd disturbed weren't trying to flee; they were bent on attacking. Instead of slowing to half-speed, Nora was only forbidden to run. In Camille's backstory, she'd nearly been turned in Mexico, then was saved by locals who drove away the vampire feeding on her. She'd become something that was neither human nor vampire — useful to have on your side, in other words.

The battle played like any other, only with vampire teeth and useless stakes instead of foam swords and shields. The vampires didn't need weapons to give damage; all players had been told a vampire's bare hands were plenty. Brody saw Amelie/Lady Elizabeth lose one arm, then one leg, then die. The other vampire got Jaden/Kaspar by the throat and "threw" (it was really a theatrical push, which Robert assisted) him over a table. The table turned out to be a prop as well; it broke in two and dropped Kaspar to a safety mat beneath.

Brody/Virgo, meanwhile, was going for the injured woman. The vampires seemed to have forgotten her in all the killing, but being human was the pits because at half-speed it was taking him forever to reach her. It was the right move, though; he saw before reaching her that she was pulling something from a pocket, then reaching forward to give it to him.

Virgo took the object as the woman breathed her last breath and died. It seemed at first to be a fistful of loose metal, but then he realized she'd handed him two things. The first was a small crucifix. The other was a ...

Holy shit. *It was a silver stake.*

One of the vampires was turning and coming for him, having felled Orlo (Shadow Stalker) and Rohit (Baron Helmut), the latter of which was still dying in grand fashion. Camille Usher looked injured; she was gripping her neck with one hand and had her other arm behind her back, apparently severed.

Brody/Virgo raised the crucifix without thinking. The vampire screeched and flinched away.

"They can't look at crosses!" he shouted. "THEY'RE VULNERABLE TO CROSSES!"

He looked around, but the only one still alive and fully functional was Robert, AKA Mack Knight. At least he was the right one to survive, given the circumstances.

It took Robert a second, but then he was reaching into his shirt to pull out Mack's huge, Crusades-era cross. Brody wasn't sure it would work; the organizers had been clear that they couldn't bring weapons. But apparently crosses weren't weapons; Robert's had been allowed and, as the other vampire hissed, appeared to work just fine.

Robert/Mack lunged and pressed his cross to the vampire's forehead. It screamed, then fell to the ground and began to writhe. Brody/Virgo kicked the vampire he'd been dueling in the chest, then rushed over and used his silver stake to impale the other. This done, he and Robert rushed toward the other with both crosses up. The vampire hissed and ran through the doorway, into the street.

Brody moved to follow, but Nora/Camille was limping over. "Let it go," she said. "Lord knows I am not up to pursuit."

"I guess I was wrong about the cross," said Rohit/Helmut from the ground. "Good thing you kept it."

"Shut up," said Brody. "You're dead."

Rohit died dramatically again.

"Night club," said Virgo Blackheart. "I told you."

His two living fellow vampire hunters nodded, humbled.

Then they sat amongst the dead and waited for their fellows, after fifteen minutes, to rise again.

SIX
MAP

While they were waiting for their team members to resurrect, Brody, Robert, and Nora began to search the scene for clues and useful items. They searched the nightclub with renewed interest now that they knew something had been there, but mostly they searched the exploded cubicle and the dead human woman covered in blood.

From the floor, officially dead, Orlo watched with interest. Anything could be a clue. He technically wasn't supposed to be doing anything, including thinking and reasoning, but it was a difficult part of his brain to shut off. Between Orlo and the "dead" woman, Amelie lay with her eyes closed, so compliant with the no-living-while-dead rule that she might be sleeping. She was pretty in a different way when she was like this, and seeing it now gave Orlo longing like a tug in the pit of his stomach. What would it be like to wake up next to her?

Amelie's eyes opened to see him staring right at her.

"What?" she whispered.

"Shh. We're dead."

Orlo closed his eyes long enough to know obedient

Amelie had surely closed hers, then opened his again. This time he looked at the dead woman. He made himself forget he was Orlo Goldman and made himself think as Shadow Stalker. As a cop, Shadow had fine deductive powers indeed.

The woman was in her lower twenties and wearing a smartly-cut white dress, her look somewhere between a sacrificial virgin and a Forever 21 model. Blood covered her front, most abundant at the neck. One hand dangled. Blood dripped from the end of her limp fingers. Brody, who wasn't dead, was giving her a quick once-over with his eyes. Seeing something, he reached down and fumbled where the woman's belt would be.

The dead woman laughed. Brody, who'd tickled her, muttered, "Sorry." He went to move her, then whisper-asked if she'd prefer to move herself. He nodded when neither thing happened: the woman just said quietly, "There's nothing under me." It wasn't exactly to protocol and honestly kind of broke the mood, but that was Brody for you. If he searched the dead girl using his hands, it might feel like intrusive. Like he was crossing a line.

"Guild of mine," said Nora in her Camille voice. "I've found something." She'd regained use of her limbs and was no longer limping. As a half-vampire, Camille healed faster than mortals.

There were only two living members of her clan for the next two minutes or so, but those two went to her. Orlo noticed that Brody had tucked their first weapon — that shining silver stake — into his belt.

"What do you make of it, Kaspar?" Nora asked Jaden.

Orlo tried to see what they were talking about, but he'd have to sit up to do it. He waited, eyes on the clock.

They discussed, but Orlo couldn't hear. The conversation seemed to end without satisfaction. Rohit sat up first, then said loudly in Baron Helmut von Baden's voice, *"Das ist glorious not to be dead!"* There was technically a minute left, but with the bubble popped, Orlo went ahead and sat up anyway.

"Ah, Shadow Stalker. You live again."

"And you as well, Kaspar," Orlo returned.

He looked to greet Amelie in the same way, but Lady Elizabeth was already shuffling her wardrobe and moving in the other direction. Orlo paused to admire it — not to look at her ass, per se, but the clothing itself. Lady Elizabeth Jane Warwick's get-up looked like starched petticoats and bone corsets, but he'd seen her move in similar medieval gear enough to know her typical wear wasn't restrictive at all: Lady Elizabeth, whether she was a vampire hunter or a kick-ass bar maiden, could run swiftly and kick high without so much as exposing her knickers. He'd complimented her seamstress abilities often, but to his own ears such praise always sounded pathetic.

Now they were huddled around Camille Usher, who was once again looking as badass as ever. Orlo joined them to find a discussion already in progress.

Camille/Nora was holding a piece of weathered paper upon which had been drawn a glyph of some kind. She told them the dead girl had been clutching it in one hand.

"The sun?" said Lady Elizabeth, looking.

Kaspar Ripley shook his head. "If it's the sun, what are all these here? I think it looks more like the Nazca Lines or something."

"Vat are Nascar Lines?" asked Helmut von Baden.

"Nazca," Kaspar clarified.

"Why the hell would vampires care about the Nazca Lines?" asked Camille Usher.

"Und who ze hell vould know vat zey are?" said Helmut.

"You know," said Kaspar. "Lines made by UFOs."

But Orlo wasn't buying any of those interpretations. "It's a map," he said.

They all looked from the paper to him.

"It's a map of the ..." He was about to say "convention center," but caught himself and said, "town" instead. Game lore said that all of this was taking place in a tiny New England town west of Boston, population twenty thousand. It was the Game Master's attempt to give them a compromise between a small, old-feeling setting and that of a full-on city, which they couldn't re-create without the whole thing looking dumb.

"We already have a map. Why would she have a map?"

"I don't know, but look." Orlo took the paper from Nora/Camille and turned it ninety degrees, pointing at landmarks as he named them. "This is the city gate. This is town hall. This right here is the club we're in now. Remember coming through the ..." He had to think, but then he had it. "... the general store, here?"

They all looked with renewed interest. Two locations on the hand-drawn and unlabeled map were connected with a line that appeared not to be part of the map itself. To Orlo, it looked like instructions: start here, go there.

"Too obvious," said Virgo Blackheart. "Why would the vampires literally draw a map, like, 'Hey, come look for us here!'" But Brody's turn to lead was over. He'd been right about avoiding the catacombs and trying the club instead, but sometimes *obvious*, in games like this, was the only way.

"It vas in her hand," said Helmut von Baden. "Maybe *she* iz ze one who drew it?"

That was good enough for Orlo. "The theater, then."

The others deferred so he could go first, and then the entire guild followed behind, out of the club and onto their next phase.

When they were gone, the first referee looked to the second.

"Should we tell them they read it wrong?" he asked.

The second shook her head. "The theater's locked and the auditorium is right next door. They'll figure it out."

SEVEN

WHAT'S YOUR NAME?

Jaden was fully Kaspar Ripley. In truth, he seldom wanted to be anything else. Kaspar was his real self, and Jaden was the mask.

Nobody ever believed Jaden about anything other than what boring old human eyes could see and the boring old human mind could logically conceive. By contrast, *everyone* believed Kaspar because Kaspar lived in a magical world and magic was all around him. Today Kaspar was uncovering a vampire conspiracy. Last weekend and most weekends, Kaspar was a sorcerer. There were no questions, in-game and in-world, about what Kaspar could do and what Kaspar knew as fact. Yet as an everyday human child, Jaden Grey had seen supernatural things, told his parents, and then endured supervised therapy — and, for a while, anti-psychotic medication that put a haze over everything. It had only ended when Jaden pretended to be cured. He told his parents he understood why he *thought* he'd seen those things, and knew now that they weren't real. He even told them some of what he'd said were lies, told just to get attention.

But telling his parents he'd lied? *That* was the real lie.

What Jaden had seen as a kid — and then several times afterward — was real. Jaden was sure of it. He knew because it was so specific: He didn't see *all* sorts of crazy things, just *one specific* crazy thing. Despite an interest in UFOs, Jaden didn't see aliens. Despite his interest in ESP, he didn't hear voices. Those things were just hobbies. He maybe believed them and maybe didn't, in the way any curious young man would.

But ... supernatural beings? About *them*, Jaden was sure. He still remembered being ten, being twelve, being fifteen — and then and now, seeing things that shouldn't be possible.

At ten years old, he'd seen two men crouch at the back of the alley that ran behind his house, then jump directly onto a three-story roof. One, he'd have sworn, had then turned into a small black thing and flown away.

At twelve, he'd seen a convenience store robbery from inside his parents' car. They were inside; Jaden was in the backseat waiting. A shirtless, dirty man had entered the store. Jaden didn't see him raise a knife, though his parents swore he'd had one. They also swore he'd been hopped-up on PCP because he'd leapt at one of the clerks and practically ripped his head off, and how could he have done so much damage (and moved so quickly) without weapons? The second clerk had pulled a pistol from beneath the counter, and Jaden had watched in slow motion as three red blooms appeared not just in the robber's chest, but through his back as well. There was no question of a bulletproof vest because he was shirtless, and in Jaden's mind there was also no question the slugs had struck his heart, his lungs, or both. Yet the man had run away at top speed (okay: much *more* than top speed), crashing through the glass front of the store without slowing. He ran right past Jaden, by which time all his wounds had healed. After passing the car, he'd seemed to disappear. He ran so fast, it was like something out of an old Looney Tunes cartoon.

Time and time again, Jaden saw things science could not explain, all centered on what looked like normal people who only came out at night. It felt like they were stalking him. As if one day, he'd find a powder-white face at the window, tapping to be let in.

He'd told his guild none of this. They, like anyone else, would think him crazy. The guild knew only that Jaden was very steeped in monster lore, and that he had a particular interest in vampires. It was Jaden who'd wanted to do vampire LARP in the past, and it was Jaden who'd found this tournament. He felt, on some level, that he needed it. Playing a vampire hunter was cathartic. It made him feel (falsely, but did it really matter?) that if the undead came, at least he'd have the experience of battle.

As Shadow Stalker led the guild through the simulated town to the theater, Kaspar Ripley felt goosebumps form on Jaden Grey's skin. He was suddenly a hybrid of both people: His real-world self combined with his character. He had Kaspar's cunning and confidence, but also Jaden's sense of imminent danger. He hadn't felt it in years, but he was feeling it now. Maybe he was psychic after all.

Amelie put a hand between his shoulder blades. He was supposed to think of her as Lady Elizabeth, but he could feel Amelie's real-world concern bleeding through Lady Elizabeth's facade.

"Are you okay?"

"I'm fine, m'lady," he lied.

"You look white."

"I *am* white, m'lady."

"I mean whiter than usual. Like, sick."

Jaden let his real voice come through his character. Weaker, he said, "It's okay."

"You're sure?"

"I'm sure."

But still her eyes lingered on him. They'd known each other for a few years now, and she knew his worry from his lies. There was a reason Amelie had been able to elbow her way into an established guild that needed no new members. She was a "we" person, not an "I" person. She was kind and thoughtful, always looking out for the others. Of course she'd fit right in, assisting and comforting wherever she could.

Jaden reinforced his smile. "Really. I just ... not enough breakfast."

Their attention was stolen by Shadow Stalker, who was investigating the door to the room indicated on the map.

"It's locked," he said.

Robert pushed forward. He was all skinny arms and elbows. His manner was upright, almost artificial.

"I can pick it," he said.

"No, I mean ..." Orlo grabbed the handle and rattled the door, then spoke as Orlo instead of Shadow Stalker. "I mean it's locked for real."

"Virgo," said Nora/Camille. "Let me see that stake you got from the maiden."

Virgo handed it over. She examined the thing, trying to unscrew it and pull it apart.

"What are you doing?"

"I thought there might be a key inside."

"Wait!" said Brody/Virgo. "The crucifix!" He'd put it around his neck after driving away the remaining vampire. He pulled it out.

"Das ist nicht ein schlüssel either," Baron Helmut commented.

"Gimmie that," said Robert/Mack. He took the crucifix, jammed it into the keyhole, and wiggled. The thing wouldn't enter the crack, let alone turn.

"There must be another way," said Nora/Camille, looking around. Jaden knew the look; she was searching for a referee but didn't want to say so. Looking for refs broke the fourth wall, but game officials were the only people they could ask about aspects of the game — such as, were they allowed to invoke their character's special abilities, or were all things they needed within the game itself? Robert's character could pick any lock easily. Robert himself? Not so much.

"Maybe the woman had a key and we missed it," said Shadow Stalker.

"I searched her," Virgo told him.

"Maybe you missed something. Maybe she had it in a pocket."

"No, no ..." Jaden understood the hesitation: Brody hadn't patted her down, he'd asked her in the name of bodily courtesy. She'd said no, she had nothing more. End of story. "I'm sure she didn't have a key."

"It must be back in the room somewhere. Maybe one of the vampires has it."

"We need another way in," Camille repeated, still looking around for help. She moved away from the others, looked along the hallway, and said, "Hey! There's another door down here!"

She rushed toward it. The door there was smaller than the other and mostly concealed: probably stage access, maybe even rigging access. Not the sort of place humans would hang out, but a perfect hiding place for undead vermin.

"It's unlocked!" she said, pressing the hidden door's edge.

"Vat time is it?" the Baron asked instead of following.

"Almost 6:30am." Game time, obviously.

"Zen de sun vill be rising soon."

"So what?"

"Eet had not yet. And ze theater ..." Rohit's accent was falling apart. He always said W's with a V sound, but beyond that his Austrian was inconsistent. To Jaden's ear he often sounded French.

But Shadow Stalker understood, and completed the Baron's sentence: "It's an open-air theater," he said, remembering what they'd been told. In the real world, the place had a roof on it, but not in the world of the game. "So ... what? Does the guild think we should wait another hour for the protection of the sun?"

Lady Elizabeth shook her head. "No. The other hunter clans will be this way soon. They are skilled and will follow the path we followed. For now we have the advantage. I shall not speak for the guild, but I for one am not keen to give up our lead so quickly."

Jaden nodded, agreeing. It was taking all he had to stay in 21st century character. He kept wanting to bow and declare that his honor was being neglected, but for once they weren't in a game set in 16th century Europe. In modern-day New England, people didn't say "shall" and "keen" very often. Instead they said "fuck" and told people to put down their cell phones and get out of the way.

"Besides," said Virgo, "if we wait for daylight, the vampires inside will hide. They will be all the more dangerous once driven to the shadows."

"I agree," said Camille. "It is what the vampire half of my blood longs to do."

"Okay, then," said Shadow Stalker. "We go."

They moved to the door. Lady Elizabeth had her fingers just inside, holding it open. "Be wary," she said, and then all seven of them stepped through the door.

It was dark. They had, as Jaden figured, emerged into the underside of the stage, opposite the large round room from the primary doors. The stage was raised here; he could look up and see it overhead. Once in, he lifted an arm to look at his watch, then did the time translation. It was as they'd said outside: nearly time for fake sunrise. There were still at least ten real-world minutes left before the sun broke the game's horizon, but he'd still have expected lights inside to have begun warming, simulating the purple-cum-blue that foretold the beginning of night's end. Instead, Jaden saw no colors — no light at all. Maybe the stage was a more complete barrier than he'd thought. Maybe, though it seemed he should be able to see the theater's ceiling between gaps in the stage, he actually couldn't.

Still, it made his skin prickle even more than before. This was right according to the map they'd found, but it didn't feel right at all.

Jaden's foot struck something. He looked down to see a body on the floor.

"*Hunters!*" he whisper-shouted. "*Look!*"

They gathered. The body was ordinary, zero thought whatsoever put into costume. It looked like a fat stage hand with his belly flopped out, skin white with blood on his collar. Like the Baron's accent and Lady Elizabeth's over-formality, the dead workman felt sloppy. The game staff could at least have dressed him in something hip or trendy. Could at least have covered that belly, unless they'd wanted to show how white it was — how completely he'd been drained.

"A body!"

"Vampires," said Baron Helmut. "Dey are here."

"Knew it," said Shadow Stalker. "Good work, Camille."

But Jaden was wondering something. Camille had found the concealed door because she was naturally observant (as organized as the real Nora, though she was supposed to let it go when she was in character), but without her keen eyes they'd never have found a way in. A hidden door like that was exactly the kind of thing that Camille's half-blood backstory would have made obvious, though ... and yet there'd been no game officials around to tell her it was there specifically because she — and she alone — had the vampire eyes to see it. The game's correct direction should be lined with officials for just that reason: to field incoming players, then remind them of things their characters' special abilities let them see, hear, smell, or do. Yet they'd seen no officials since leaving the nightclub. If clues had led them under the theater's stage, shouldn't there be refs here to watch their progress — if only to make sure they didn't cheat?

Shadow Stalker bent down. Lady Elizabeth bent beside him. Their hands and shoulders touched. Shadow Stalker looked at Lady Elizabeth, and for just a second they were again Orlo and Amelie.

Then Camille spoke, her brown-bob haircut swinging in curtains beside her face. "Stay low. Listen."

They all listened. There was a sound. It was low, wet, and gave Jaden a shiver. He'd swear he'd heard that sound before. It was like the glide of a soaked sponge on glass. It was the drip of wet moss down a moldering wall.

Hearing it, Mack/Robert raised a hand, taking them

back to nonverbal signals. He pointed, then shrugged. It must mean he thought the sound was that way, but wasn't quite sure.

Mack and Shadow Stalker led. The others followed. Jaden alone remained behind, thinking it prudent to search the body for clues.

He looked at the man's still face. He wasn't moving even a little. Top notch, this actor.

Jaden searched the loose-flapping pockets of the man's unzipped hoodie. He looked back at the man's face, then patted his chest to see if he wore jewelry, like a necklace, that might be important. The corner of a piece of paper was protruding from his pocket like a tease, so Jaden pinched it and pulled. It was in there too well and wouldn't budge.

"I'm just going to reach into your pocket," he told the man. "Okay?"

No response. It was okay.

He reached. The fit was tight. He added a second hand and worked the denim, peeking up occasionally to make sure he wasn't being ambushed. His guild had stopped not far ahead, Mack signing for quiet. Their collective body language was tense, as if they'd found something but hadn't yet summoned the courage to approach. Maybe it was Jaden's imagination, but he'd swear that wet sound — coming from whatever his guild had gathered around — was louder now. There were nearly-sexual moans beneath it.

"Can you ... Can you roll a little?" Jaden asked the dead man. "You're kind of ... you know ... *on it.*"

He didn't want to be rude. The man was large and his body was twisted such that the pocket was smashed between his hip and the floor, but being much more specific was tantamount to calling him fat.

But the man wouldn't roll. What an asshole.

Jaden, at a third the man's weight, had to get low and wedge his foot against a stage pillar to gain enough leverage to push. He did, and the man rolled. The man refused to stay that way, though, so Jaden (now finding the volunteer uncooperative to the point of belligerence) had to wedge a shoulder against him and apply even more force to keep him upright. Meanwhile his hands were free, barely, to scavenge in the pocket.

The paper was an invoice for lighting equipment.

Jaden's face scrunched. "What the hell is th—?"

He stopped, paralyzed. He'd meant to look the man in the face, but his head had flopped in the other direction. Jaden had already begun to notice how stiff the man was, and how cold, but his senses didn't have to report that to his brain to know everything was amiss.

The back of the man's head told the rest of the story. It wasn't just covered in blood. It looked actually concave with chips of extruded bone.

It almost looked like his brain had been devoured from the outside in.

At first Jaden was so terrified, he couldn't make words. Then it all came out at once — not information so much as raw panic.

"WE HAVE TO GET OUT OF HERE! THIS GUY IS—!"

His warning died in an avalanche of shouts and screeches from the rest of the group, over by the whatever-it-was. Jaden shut his mouth, let the corpse fall, and scrambled toward standing. His balance failed; his feet slipped in a dark spot that turned out to be a massive puddle of blood. It wasn't fake blood, either. It wasn't cornstarch and water mixed with food dye. No, this smelled like copper so much that once it was in his nostrils, Jaden felt like he was biting a penny. The puddle was thick, starting to congeal at the edges.

Jaden felt bile rise, sure he'd vomit. But he couldn't vomit, because a man's face had just materialized in front of Jaden's. A man was now blocking his way, arrived as instantly as if he'd teleported.

Time seemed to stop. Jaden became aware of seconds ticking while he paused in his bubble, aware that six friends were rushing toward and past him in sudden mortal terror. He saw Rohit slip in the blood, saw Rohit recover without falling. But Jaden only barely saw it all, because he was fascinated by the new man's aura. The man was odd. Interesting. He was also, somehow, too still. Too calm. It was like being alone on a moonlit night, then realizing wolves were spying you from the shadows.

There was no breeze, and yet the man's light brown hair seemed to float and sway. He never took his eyes off of Jaden, despite the screams and shouts. His eyes were blue. Deep, fathoms-deep blue. He had a slim athletic face — the casually handsome features of an effortless athlete. He had no stubble, clean-shaven as a baby. His teeth were very white. Very straight. Except for the canines, which were lowering into points with the speed of a feather dropping.

"What's your name?" the man asked.

"Jaden."

"My name is Arek. It's nice to meet you, Jaden."

"Yes," Jaden told him.

"Say. Do you happen to know anyone named—"

Like a snap, the trance was broken. It happened when something large, heavy-sounding, and metallic entered the scene. Jaden knew it was heavy because when it collided with the handsome man's skull, it made the sound of a striker against a church-tower bell. A small cracking noise followed. The man hit the sub-stage floor and suddenly Amelie was standing over him, a huge fire extinguisher in her hand.

"What the ...?" Jaden looked at the man, who was only stunned and rousing quickly. The breaking of the spell was all that told him there'd been a spell in the first place. *"Who the hell ...?"*

Without a word, Amelie hit the stirring man again — swinging overhead this time. He went down harder, but Jaden didn't get to see how fast he recovered this time. A second after striking him, Amelie released the extinguisher and let it roll into the shadows. Then she took Jaden by the wrists and pulled. Her strength was shocking. She was one of those stories you sometimes hear, about ordinary people finding extraordinary strength to save someone pinned under a wreck.

Or, in this case, spellbound by a real-life vampire.

EIGHT
SHOW

Amelie put her back to the door and heaved giant breaths, either literally unable to move ... or completely, and from the depths of her soul, unwilling to try. But then she thought of what she and the others had seen by the stage dumbwaiter, and she thought of how quickly the two new men had moved, and she thought finally of how the forty-pound old-fashioned extinguisher had barely stopped one of them when she'd used it to break his head open. That, finally, got her up again.

She'd stopped too early; she knew that now. This situation called for much more extensive flight than simply leaving the room. This called for panic. For running around in circles, screaming at the moon. This called for drooling, for vomiting, for climbing under the covers and never coming out.

So Amelie swallowed the burning in her chest and got to her feet once more. The timing was good. If she'd waited another few seconds, she probably wouldn't have found the strength.

"That man was ... He was ..." Jaden had lost his interest in finishing sentences.

"No he wasn't," Amelie said.

"You hit him and he healed! You broke his skull!"

That wasn't all that'd happened. There was also a young woman still under the stage who'd looked vivisected — something Jaden hadn't seen. Before she'd broken her own paralysis, Amelie could've sworn she'd seen a heart still beating inside the woman's pried-open ribcage. Despite all the blood on the floor, tiny jets of gore had still managed to squirt from her neck like miniature drinking fountains with pressure issues.

Jaden hadn't seen the entirety of his part, either, Amelie figured. They'd seen the two dark men over the body; both had hissed; one had seemed to blip out of existence and reappear thirty or more feet away. Then she'd seen the man go calm, and she'd seen him eye to eye with Jaden, and she'd seen the way Jaden's head had started to wobble and his hands had gone slack, sagging down his kneeling thighs like soaked rags.

Add that to the skull-bashing, and the whole party became a giant bouquet of *what-the-fuck*.

"We need to go," Amelie said.

She didn't want to hear any more on the issue — not now, not after they kept on running. She didn't want to hear the perfectly logical insane explanation that Jaden was about to give — and she knew perfectly well that he'd give it because this was *Jaden* they were talking about, and handsome undead shadows were Jaden's explanation for everything. When he was younger he'd worn a cape, he'd told them all one night. His parents had wondered why: *Why the cape, Jaden? Does it make you a superhero?*

For camouflage. So they can't tell me from one of them.

Then the treatments. Then the pills.

Amelie dragged Jaden far as she could go before fight-or-flight hangover set in. They made it past the semicircular hallway around the theater, through the conjoined meeting rooms set up as a dive bar, down the alleyway and through the back door of the main apartment building in Vampire Dominion's fake neighborhood. Only then did she realize she'd paid no attention whatsoever to the others. She had no idea where they were. Was it more noble that she'd stopped for Jaden, or more cowardly that she'd left everyone else behind?

Something fell like the proverbial sack of potatoes beside her, on the opposite side from Jaden. She was so keyed-up, she did the only thing that occurred to her primordial brain: she grabbed a stake from the garter beneath her starched dress and slammed it into the new man's heart.

It was a LARP stake, padded for safety. It snapped the moment it struck Orlo's chest.

"It's me."

"Jesus. Jesus fucking Christ, Orlo. Don't do that to me."

"Do what to you? *Follow* you?"

"Jesus Christ. Jesus Christ." She couldn't stop calling for her savior. She took back everything she'd said, to her mother or grandmother, about church's abject dumbness. All that mattered now was for her heart to keep on beating. Everything else — food, sanity, the sun's continued existence — mattered a distant second.

She jumped again, screaming this time. But now it was Brody whose coat brushed her ankles.

"Shit, Lady Elizabeth!" Brody said. "Chill out!"

"Move your foot. Move your foot. *YOU'RE ON MY LEGS!*" It wasn't more than a passing brush, but suddenly

Brody keeping his foot near her ankle was freaking Amelie right the fuck out. It was all she could focus on, because if she stopped focusing on Brody's violation of her personal space, she'd have to cede mental ground to whatever-the-hell just happened in there.

She wasn't breathing, unless occasional dizzying gasps counted as breath. She also wasn't thinking; this was more like the "thought" a cockroach did while trying to avoid the blow of a shoe. *Calm down. Calm down.* Her saying it to herself was actually working. *Just keep your head in the game. Just put your game face on. Keep a stiff upper lip. Stay calm and carry on, just like the queen.*

Brody moved the offending foot. "Okay! Okay, you're good!"

"I'm not kidding you, Brody!"

"Hey! It's 'Virgo Blackheart'!"

"DON'T FUCKING GIVE ME THAT GAME SHIT RIGHT NOW DON'T YOU DARE!"

Brody backed away with his hands up, palms out, eyes so wide she may as well have been a bomb he was trying to disarm.

"What's wrong with you?"

"What's wrong with *me*? Didn't you see what was going on in there?"

"Yeah, and it was super rad!" Brody looked around. Everyone was here, at least; Amelie's head had cleared enough to register that much. Nobody responded so Brody looked at each one in turn, waiting for an answer that seemed increasingly unlikely to come. Finally he said, "What's going on with you guys?"

"That wasn't acting." It was Robert, not Mack Knight. Robert, like Amelie, seemed about as far from his LARP character right now as a person could be.

"Of course it was acting!" Brody said.

Another pause. Brody waited for support. Again none came.

"Seriously?" he tried. "We hit the motherlode and now you guys wanna back off and run away?"

"What 'motherlode,' Brody?" asked Rohit.

"Stop calling me Brody! My name is Virgo Blackheart!"

"This is serious!" said Nora.

"How is it serious?" Brody wasn't really asking anymore. He was incredulous: a sane man surrounded by crazies.

"Those men were eating that woman alive!"

"They're *ACTORS!* This is a *GAME!* What, you run screaming from haunted houses, too?"

"How can you think that was fake?" Nora asked.

"How can *you* think it was *real?*" He turned to Orlo and leaned in: one rational man appealing to his only rational ally. "Shadow Stalker. *Orlo.* You know all about special effects. You get that what we saw in there was fake, right?"

Orlo looked unsure.

"Come on, man. Fake or real, what did you see? Go ahead and say it."

Orlo paused, then did as Brody asked. "Vampires. Feeding on a woman."

"Okay. What game are we playing? Come on. What's its name?"

Orlo looked at Amelie like a boy caught stealing. Slowly he said, "'Vampire Dominion.'"

"Just stop and think, okay?" Now Brody was talking to all of them. "We went in looking for vampires. *We found vampires.* We were all excited about that exact thing before ... well, before *whatever* happened when you all started yelling and running. Because we'd found them, right?" He turned to Rohit. "Rohit. You even said, before we saw shit: 'Ze vampires. Zere are vampires here.' Remember that?"

When again nobody replied, Brody threw his hands in the air and gave up completely. "Guys! This is a *vampire game!* And you saw *vampires!* Do you really think that's strange?"

"If they were *real*, it's strange!" Amelie was actually growing more upset the longer Brody talked, not less. She hadn't yet worked out why.

"They're not real! There's no such thing as vampires!"

Now they were all looking to each other, less scared and more confused.

Brody continued. "Are you really freaked out over a really great practical effect? Come on! This is the biggest and most elaborate live multiplayer game I've ever heard of! Will you think about it, just for two seconds?" He seemed flabbergasted that he was even having to say any of this. "Seriously. They rented out an *entire three-floor conference center,* charged *nine hundred bucks a head,* and spread things out over *three full days.* Usually we get ... what ... five, six hours total? Are you really so shocked there'd be decent special effects at something like this?"

Nobody protested right away this time.

"Guys," Brody said in something more like his normal voice, placing a firm and sensible hand flat on the floor like a foundation anchor. "This is really flattering for the organizers, I'm sure. Maybe you should go to the Game Master area and give them a testimonial. What do you think — huh, Jaden? How 'bout you, Rohit? You're nor shy. *'I was so freaked out by ze effects in Vampire Dominion, I almost forfeited my entry fee and ran off to call the cops!'* They show that online and people will *beg* them to take their money."

"But ... We all saw ...." Nora sounded like she wanted to

believe him, but just couldn't. She turned to Orlo. "Could they really make something look that real with special effects? I mean, outside of a movie?"

Before Orlo could answer, Brody sighed. "This is what we paid for. Everyone got that? On the ride up, we were all saying, 'I hope they can make it scary.' 'I hope they make it look good.' 'I hope it's not all cardboard sets and some assholes walking around like, 'I *vant* to *suck* your *blood!*' Anyone but me remember that?" Then he looked at Amelie and frowned at the look on her face. "What?"

Amelie looked at Jaden.

"What did *you* see?" she asked him.

"I don't know. I'm not sure."

"Think. You weren't with the rest of us. You found something and you yelled out. Before I came over and ..." She swallowed; saying the next thing too soon would be putting a rather unfortunate cart before a rather unfortunate horse. "Before I came over, what did you see?"

"That guy on the floor. He was dead. Like actually dead. But ..."

Jaden trailed off as he traded glances with Amelie. She'd seen the man in question only briefly, but her moment's memory had shown her a mangled body. She couldn't remember, right now, how exactly it'd been mangled. In the moment, it had confirmed what she'd already seen, with the vivisected woman. Now, though, she wasn't so sure. And that was a very bad thing, if Brody was right.

"*What*, Amelie?" Now it was Jaden who asked.

"If it wasn't real, I ..."

"You what?"

She closed her eyes. She saw the heavy swing of the fire extinguisher. Heard the smash of metal on bone. But that wasn't enough, was it? Because she hadn't just hit the guy once. After he'd staggered upright, she'd done it again. Harder the second time, overhead like an axe through firewood.

"We have to go back."

"What? *Why?*" It was Orlo. He'd looked ready to believe Brody, but that agreement was on intellectual grounds. If he had to put his money where his mouth had so recently been, he seemed prepared to be terrified all over again.

"Because if what happened back there was all just for show," Amelie said, "I think I may have killed someone."

NINE

RATS

JJ looked down at his maker. The girl had done quite a number on him. Whatever she'd hit with (he hadn't seen what it was; he'd been preoccupied trying to pick up the rat carcasses he'd spilled) had broken the bone at the top of his nose, bending the whole works inward. Arek's eyes, comically, ended up looking at one another.

Those bits of broken-in skull had also impaled his brain's frontal lobe. Right now he was little more than an animal. He'd remain that way until his body healed, his re-forming brain pushing bone and skin and blood back where it belonged. Right now, though, Arek wouldn't be able to add two and two. Right now, if JJ dragged him to the front door, he could probably get Arek to walk into the sun of his own free will.

The window of opportunity ended. Arek's skull resumed its usual shape with a wet snapping sound. He blinked, coming around, then stood.

"That hurt," he said.

"It *looked* like it hurt."

"How many times did she hit me?"

"Twice, I think," said JJ. He looked at the spot where they'd been feeding when the humans approached. It was awash with blood (mostly rat blood), but otherwise empty. "Where's your lunch?" he asked.

Arek looked. "She should be here." Then he saw the woman walking around, wandering instead of laying where he'd put her — testament to Arek's terrible glamouring skills. Twin puncture wounds oozed on her neck. He yelled, "Hey! Come over here a sec, will you?"

The girl came forward slowly, like someone asleep. Arek looked her in the eye, opened his mouth, then turned to face JJ before speaking to her.

"You're sure you don't want any?"

"Thirty years. Thirty years, it's been since I've had human blood."

"Yeah, but we may be here a while. You're going to get hungry and there are only so many rats."

"Don't be so sure. This is Detroit."

"I just thought, given the circumstances ..."

"I'm a vampire, Arek. That doesn't mean I have to be a monster."

Arek rolled his eyes as if JJ had just announced his belief in fairies. To the girl he said, "You wandered into a restricted area. You slipped and fell in some stage blood. You got it all over your virgin costume, so now you need to change."

"Stage blood," she repeated.

"It smelled like dead rats for some reason."

JJ sighed. "Humans can't smell what you smell."

"Good," Arek said, wrinkling his nose, "because it's vile. Nobody should eat rats. Not even ... What eats rats?"

"Courteous vampires."

"Yeah. Them and Bigfoot. The hills are alive with

both." He looked back at the girl and said, "Tell anyone who asks that you cut your neck when you fell. You're sorry, but you have to back out of volunteering for the rest of today because you feel sort of sick. A little weak. So when you get home, eat a cookie."

"And spinach," said JJ.

Arek looked back.

"For the iron," JJ clarified.

"Call off tomorrow," Arek told the girl. "Do whatever suits you, but come back for Day Three. Come *here*—" He patted the air, indicating this exact spot. "—again at noon on Sunday. Oh. And wash your neck this time."

"I'm tired," the girl said.

"You never met either of us."

The girl nodded and walked away. When she was gone, both vampires looked back where Arek had been feeding. The blood and rat corpses JJ had accidentally slopped from his bucket had mostly hit her chest. Spillage had splashed around her, leaving the inverse outline of a body.

"You're going to clean that up," said Arek.

"I was in the middle of cleaning it up."

"You ruined my last few sips. You understand that, right? I really wanted to take my time. Fuel up good before we went back out there. Then some shitpot spills dead rats all over my meal"

"Maybe if you hadn't laid her right in the middle of the goddamn walkway ..."

"Hey. Asshole." Arek puffed up. "I'm the one doing things the right way here. You're the one crawling around under the floorboards, collecting rodents. You know, I don't get you. You don't want to feed on people? Fine. But these kids, in this game? They're asking for it. They've got one of the rooms set up like some sort of modern opium den. Big old hookah, and these kids are practically fucking in a circle around it. Dorks playing vampires, dorks playing victims. It's all fun for them. The girls here, they *want* dudes sucking on their necks."

"It's not just about consent," said JJ. "Haven't you ever met a vegetarian? Some people make choices, you know."

"Vegetarians were called something else when I was alive."

"What?"

"'Pussies,'" said Arek. He shook his head. This was an intolerable situation. If only his progeny hadn't disappointed him, like so many sons letting down so many fathers. "Where's your suck sack?"

"If you're referring to my CamelBak, I drank it all already."

Arek gave up. If JJ wanted to drink Kosher blood and rats, that was his business.

JJ was looking toward the stage door, closing behind the departing girl. He said, "What did you tell that kid before the girl hit you?"

"Nothing."

"Nothing?"

"I didn't get a chance. I was going to ask about Arcadia when she clocked me."

JJ waved it all away, resetting on this rather large mistake Arek had made. "Wait. So you *didn't* give him a story to tell his friends? You saw how they screamed. They thought we were killing her. They're going to report it. Are you saying you *didn't* get a chance to glamour him out of snitching?"

Arek nodded slowly. "Uh-huh. So I assume *you* glamoured the *other* five or six of them? *I'm* the only one who left loose ends?"

JJ sat heavily. Arek was right; the mistake was both of theirs and now they'd have to find a way to fix it. The problem was, Arek only planned about fifteen minutes ahead, and mistakes tended to thrive that way. If it was up to JJ, they'd always think things through and never run off half-cocked. JJ actually *liked* to plan, and did so within the rather large margin of error introduced by Arek's lack of forethought.

"Okay," JJ said. "Here's what we do. We go after them."

"I don't want to go after them."

"We find at least one of them, glamour him or her, and give them a really convincing version of events to tell the others so they don't raise an alarm." JJ snapped his fingers. "I know. Go get that girl."

"Which girl?"

"The one you were … Oh, forget it." It was easier to just do it himself.

JJ ran to the door in one partial second, peeked out, then circuited the empty corridor the next second. There was no sign of the woman Arek had fed on. He returned to Arek in less than the time it'd take for something dropped from the theater's ceiling to hit the floor. "She's gone. But we can find her, too, and we can tell *her* to find *them*. Once they see her and see that she's alive, the rest won't matter. She'll tell them it was all just part of the game they're playing. They'll decide they didn't see anything interesting and get on with their lives."

"I've got a better idea," said Arek.

"What?"

"Hang on."

He'd been sitting on one of his hands. He pulled it out. The hand seemed to be on backwards. Arek grimaced, then clenched his teeth while the bones straightened and mended.

"Where were we?" he asked when it was finished. Then: "Oh. Right. Your idea is decent. But here's a counter-proposal: I say we go after the girl."

"The one you were feeding on?"

"No. The one who hit me."

"What about her?"

"She had red hair."

"Yeah. Apparently redheads are as fiesty as people say. You should have seen her form when she was beating you to death."

"The woman I had sex with right before I was turned had red hair."

"I see. So this is a fetish thing with you?" JJ couldn't believe it. Just like Arek to propose fucking when there was work to be done.

Arek shook it away. "You're missing my point. Red hair is recessive. They're like five percent of the population."

"So?"

"What was it they called her?"

"'Lady' something."

"No. They called her something else. Started with an A. I'm thinking maybe ... 'Arcadia'?"

JJ stopped. "Wait. You think she's the one we're looking for? That's a hell of a guess, considering we don't know what she looks like." Arek's great great granddaughter had turned out to be a bit of a philistine. She didn't seem to have any photos online at all, and it was hard to search for a needle in a haystack when you didn't know what a needle looked like. JJ had ideas to figure it out, but Arek apparently planned to wing it, hoping they'd get lucky.

He said, "You know how recessive genes work. Natural

redheads must have redheads in their family history. If my woman was a redhead and we know 'Arcadia' is at this tournament, logic says she'd have red hair, too."

"Actually ..." JJ said. Logic didn't say that at all. It might work the other way around, but Arek had never been a big intellectual. He was more a "shove dorks into the mud and step on them" sort of guy.

"That girl is as good a place as any to start," said Arek. "I still have a little blood memory from the girl I was feeding on, so I know she saw where the redhead went. Which door she went through, anyway."

JJ shook his head. "That's one step above random. We do this randomly and we'll screw it up. Look. There's a few hundred kids here. Any one of the girls could be her. I told you. This is really simple. You know her name's Arcadia. You know she's registered for this tournament. So we go to the organizers. We glamour them and ask who Arcadia is."

"I tried that. There are no pictures attached to the registrations. And as you so astutely pointed out, there are hundreds of people here, so nobody noticed who's who unless they had a reason, and nobody did. We tried it your way, but she's not on Facebook. Not on LifeLyfe. I don't know what she looks like, and talking to the organizers here won't change that." He pointed at his head. "Red hair. That's as good a start as any."

There was a sound. Light beams pierced the darkness. Someone had just come back through the stage door with a flashlight, or several someones. The new arrivals were talking loudly, not trying to be quiet. JJ heard no stage voices, no put-on characters, and that meant this was real-world real, not part of the game. They could slice-and-dice whoever it was — or just glamour them — but even if JJ wanted to do so (he didn't; this was Arek's errand and JJ was only here because his maker bond compelled him), it would complicate things quickly.

For now, they only had one loose end: the seven young people who'd run out of here screaming. If they acted without thinking, there'd soon be more ... and *then* how would Arek find the blood relative he needed? JJ would be okay with Arek failing, but the problem was that Arek wouldn't just *give up* when the going got tough. Failing to find "Arcadia" at the LARP tournament would just prolong the errand, and prolong JJ's obligation to be part of it. If they didn't find the girl here, he'd never be free. Arek would drag him around the globe, looking for her forever and ever.

"Security guards," Arek said, his fangs descending.

But JJ put a hand on his maker's chest. "Not yet," he said.

TEN

LIGHTS ON

Nora watched Orlo attempt to take Amelie by the arm. Amelie let him, then shook him off when she realized he was practically hugging her.

Amelie liked Orlo just fine; she just didn't like him the way everyone else — everyone but Amelie — knew he liked her. They even had an arrangement, and if you knew the score, the irony of that arrangement was downright painful. Amelie tended to attract a lot of male attention, what with those pretty features and fire-red hair of hers. You'd think LARPers, most of whom weren't confident by nature, would leave her alone, but instead the opposite was true. In an all-geek environment, guys tended to pony up, grow a pair, and act the way life's jocks usually prevented them from acting. It should have been inspiring, but instead it was creepy: all those awkward men trying to flirt and coming off like rapists instead. So the deal was, whenever Amelie was besieged, Orlo was supposed to come over and pretend to be her boyfriend. She'd fawn on him, run her fingers up and down his arm, and cuddle up close with her boobs pressed against him. Then when the offender was gone, she'd let go and return Orlo to the Friend Zone. It was painful to watch.

Thus dismissed, Orlo tried to be gallant. He moved to re-enter the sub-stage area behind the guards and in front of Amelie, but she shoved past him. Amelie didn't want to be kept, or protected, or even really supported. Her independent streak was so strong, Nora suspected it came from damage: beautiful Amelie with a flaw after all. Maybe Daddy didn't love her, and now she'd learned to trust nobody.

Stop it, Nora, she told herself. *Amelie is your friend.*

And she was. Nora didn't like being jealous. She hated it, actually. It was evidence that she, not Amelie, was the one with issues, but it came up time and time again anyway. Nora had been part of the guild for a full year before anyone knew Amelie. Back then she'd been the only girl, and even then Orlo had seen her only as a human spreadsheet. Not a woman at all.

"*Where* did you say you saw something?" the guard asked.

He'd asked Brody, but Brody refused to answer. Instead he looked to Amelie or Jaden to answer the guard, which Amelie then did. Brody was here under protest. He kept swearing that it was all theatrics — just part of the game. Orlo, who usually broke deadlocks in the group, said it was better safe than sorry. Brady had moaned mightily, but still they'd found the guards, sacrificing a sure lead for a dubious sense of danger. Amelie's fear that she'd murdered someone seemed worth investigation to Nora, but Brody apparently saw it as no big deal.

Really, Nora supposed, *nobody* was being too logical today.

The lights came on all at once. Nora flinched, but it was

just one of the guards finding a light switch they'd missed the first time.

Amelie's mouth hung open. The guards didn't react, now pacing between foundation pillars as if there might still be something hiding. The security guards didn't know what they'd all seen before — didn't know that, with that one quick flip of a switch, they'd seen all they'd need to see. Which was nothing. Nothing at all. There was no body where they'd nearly tripped over it, and there was no enormous pool of blood, no woman with glistening red guts all over her chest. No vampires, real or artificial ... not even a bloodied fire extinguisher.

"You said over there?" the second guard asked, pacing wide.

"It ... it was here."

"What was?"

"The body. A man's body was *right here.*" Amelie pointed. Despite having clear sight lines in all direction, she began to pace and circle, certain somehow that the bodies and creatures were hiding behind one of the many two-inch metal poles.

Orlo was bending over, examining the place where Nora swore there'd been a blood puddle the size of Texas. He touched the concrete, then looked at his fingertips.

"This is wet."

"With blood?" Then, because the entire thing was starting to feel foolish, Rohit corrected himself: "I mean, *fake* blood?"

"It's water," Orlo answered.

"There you go," said one of the guards. "Just water."

"It wasn't water," Jaden told them.

"You said the lights were off when you were in here before?" asked the second guard.

Orlo nodded.

"And you never turned them on?"

"We didn't see the switch," Robert said.

"Water," the second guard said to the first.

"What about the bodies?" Nora asked.

"Good question," said the first guard. "What *about* the bodies?"

Nora didn't answer. The scene around them spoke for itself. The lower-stage area wasn't large and wasn't in any way obstructed. With the lights on, there were no corners in which to hide. The place was clean — no denying it. Nora had been sure of what she'd seen, but now she was starting to doubt it.

"Look," said the first guard. "I get why this game would freak you out. It freaks *me* out. But as you can see, there's nobody here."

"Someone cleaned it up," Amelie said.

"Come on, Amelie," Brody replied. "It's been like five minutes."

"You saw it, too!"

"I saw *special effects*. My explanation doesn't require dragging away two bodies." He peeked where Orlo was standing. "Maybe they had a tarp down or something. The blood was on the tarp. We freaked out; they got up and walked away and took the tarp with them."

"There wasn't a tarp," Amelie growled.

"Guys, you're not supposed to be in here anyway," said the second guard. "The theater's being painted and should have been marked out-of-bounds on the map they gave you. Someone forgot to lock the stage door, is all. I get it. In the dark, when you're into the game, your mind invents all kinds of things."

"*I didn't make it up!*" Amelie looked around at the others like abject betrayers. "All of you saw it!"

"I ..." Orlo shrunk when Amelie turned a fiery gaze in his direction, but spoke on anyway. "I don't really know what I saw. It freaked me out at the time, but ... I don't know. Maybe it was just some people sneaking in to make out."

"Are you *shitting* me? Are you *fucking shitting* me?" She looked like she was inches from a conniption — and an indignant one at that. "Come on, Orlo! They were *right here*, and there was no tarp, and there were guts all over the place! And the guy, the one Jaden—"

"*Then where are they now, Amelie?*" Orlo never stood up to her, never. It was part of his secret courtship, Nora assumed, and the fact that he was shouting now said more than anything else. "Okay, I thought I saw something, too. But that doesn't change the fact that there's *nothing here!*"

Amelie put her hands on her hips and looked away. The first guard glanced at her turned back, then said more quietly. "You guys go on. Maybe take a break, get some water, then get back to your game. We'll lock up here. This whole thing isn't really my bag, but it looks pretty fun, right?" He'd turned to his partner, who nodded. Neither looked like they actually thought it was fun, but Nora appreciated them trying to soothe nerves, to be nice.

The guards moved away and most of the guild went for the door into the hallway. Amelie still hadn't moved.

"Look on the bright side," Nora told her. "At least you didn't kill anyone."

Amelie turned her head.

"The one thing we can be sure *wasn't* fake was you clocking that guy with the extinguisher," Nora went on.

"But look around." They both did. "Nobody. *No body*. So he couldn't have been that hurt, could he?"

Nora heard the dissonance in her own voice. On a strictly linguistic level, her words all made sense. But on a deeper, more investigative level, even her own assessment was a contradiction. There *was* no body, but there was also no extinguisher. They *did* know Amelie had hit a guy — that much, everyone agreed on. So where was the weapon? And atop that, Nora was quite sure she'd seen the aftermath: the man's head so incredibly bludgeoned by the thing, it'd changed shape. Even if her eyes had deceived her about the rest of the scene, denying the beating didn't hold water. How had someone that badly hurt gotten up and walked away without leaving so much as a drop of blood? And even if he had walked away, why had he taken the fire extinguisher with him?

"This is wrong," Amelie said, letting Nora lead her out from under the stage — to the door where the guards now stood waiting to lock back up.

Nora, though she said nothing, couldn't help but agree.

ELEVEN

DECOY

There was nothing she could do.

Amelie remained sure of what she'd seen longer than the rest — probably because if she'd seen right (and she knew she had), a homicide hung in the balance. The weight of it was like the weight of the old fire extinguisher. In the moment she'd swung the thing, she'd been so sure she'd seen something real that she'd have bet her life on it. Which, sort of, she had. They'd all seen those two men bent over the woman, one biting her neck and the other with his hands in her spilled guts. They'd seen how quickly the men moved when spotted — how fast the shorter of the two had zipped toward Jaden. Amelie alone had seen the way Jaden and the vampire were looking into each other's eyes, the former hypnotized by the latter. She wasn't a violent person. She'd only struck because she'd been *so sure* it was life and death. Those weren't actors they'd seen, and the fact that the theater was out-of-bounds only sharpened that point.

Everyone wanted to believe the four people they'd seen under the stage were up to anything but death, but Amelie still wasn't buying. The vampires' teeth had looked far too good for that. Too genuinely sharp. The blood had been too real. She was absolutely positive ... and *had* to be, in order to let time march forward. The alternative was a conscience weight down by lead. The alternative was Amelie in prison, for manslaughter at least.

"Jaden."

Jaden looked at her as they walked. There were only seven in the guild, but some friendships formed more readily than others. She and Jaden had never been close. They'd never really been alone together.

"Yeah?"

"What did you see under there?"

He shrugged. "I don't know what I saw."

"You can tell me the truth."

"I am. I don't know anymore. I thought I did, but I guess I'm wrong."

Amelie knew the feeling. The entire situation felt like gaslighting. She remained certain of everything, but the six other people who'd seen pretty much the same kept telling her she was wrong. It was hard, no matter how sure she was, to hold a diametrically opposed view. In the thirty minutes since they'd left the stage (two full game-hours, wasted), she'd begun wondering if the pictures inside her head might, somehow, be wrong — but believing that felt like someone trying to convince her that her birthday wasn't her birthday. She was dead sure, but the longer she held her certainty and the others didn't, the less sure she became.

"Tell me what you *think* you saw, then."

Still Jaden hesitated. He wasn't a bold man, and preferred the safety of going with the crowd.

"Just pretend we both know it's a dream," Amelie encouraged him.

He nodded. "Okay. Then ... I *thought* I saw vampires. Real ones."

"Why did you think that?"

"Because that guy on the floor was dead, not acting. He had a neck wound and it was like all the blood had been sucked out of him. He was cold and stiff and his head was ... empty." Pause. "But I guess maybe it wasn't a person. Maybe it was a prop, and I just thought it was a dead guy."

Amelie wasn't buying it. Up close, even special effects dummies were clearly dummies. This one had been real. But she just nodded so Jaden would go on.

"Why else?"

"The one I was talking to. The man?"

Amelie knew he'd wanted to say "the vampire" but was holding back. She waited for more.

"That guy moved so fast ..."

Amelie had seen that too. "And?"

"And when he talked to me, it was like I started going to sleep."

"Like he was glamouring you."

"Well ... yeah."

"Tell me the truth, Jaden. You've seen vampires before, right?" Then, when Jaden hesitated, Amelie pushed harder. "It's okay. You can tell me. I believe you." She never had before, but things had changed. She meant it this time.

"A few times," Jaden told her.

"Why have you seen them multiple times, do you think? I mean, most people never see them once." She wanted her question to sound Devil's-advocate, not actually doubtful. She must have done it right because Jaden didn't hesitate. He probably relished the opportunity, for once, to say what he'd always believed was true.

"I started looking for them. Most people refuse to see

what they can't explain, but strange goings-on are every-where for the believers."

Ain't that the truth. Even now, even though Amelie was certain about what she'd seen, her head kept refusing to believe. The desire to turn away was intensely strong — almost a survival instinct.

She had one more thing to ask, and then she'd let him rest. "Jaden, compared to the vampires you saw in the past, did these two seem—?"

"Hey! Up here! You guys!"

It was Brody. He'd stopped walking at the pack's lead, and now he was just a handful of feet from Amelie and Jaden. His face was split into a wide grin, but the grin fell away when he saw them. Orlo, Nora, Robert, and Rohit had by now come mostly around to the world of convenient beliefs, sure in some odd way that they'd seen nothing and eager to never think of it again. Seeing the conspiratorial looks on Amelie and Jaden's faces knocked down Brody's mirth. It was the look of a man who thought a problem had been solved — and then here it was, all over again.

"What are you guys talking about?" he asked.

"Nothing," said Jaden.

Amelie, who didn't mind letting the others know she didn't plan to let it go so easily, said nothing. She just met Brody's eyes.

Robert arrived behind them. In his Mack Knight voice, he said, "Lo, Virgo! What makes you ..."

Then he saw Amelie.

He finished in Robert-voice, his exuberance melted like snow: "... speak?"

There was a moment of tense silence. Then, starting slow and keeping his eyes on Amelie, Brody said, "I found something."

"What?" said Orlo.

Still watching Amelie, he said, "It has to do with the game. Are we still playing the game?"

"Yeah, of course," said Orlo.

"All of us?"

There was a long moment while Brody and Amelie faced off. Then she took a breath and said, "What did you find?"

"Car keys."

"So? Someone dropped them."

"They have an insignia on them. Look." He held up a chain with just three things on it: a large microchip key with a black plastic grip, a second key that was all metal, and a leather fob bearing the logo of something unknown.

Nora took the keychain. She looked around. They were in a small room with literally nowhere to hide. The keys had just been in the floor of the room, obvious to anyone.

"No one's been through here," she said. "Otherwise someone would already have found them."

"So we're in the lead again," said Rohit.

"Or we're on the wrong path," said Orlo. He took the keys and bounced them in his palm, spending extra time examining the fob. It looked like another glyph: vampire language. "This could be a decoy."

"It *is* a decoy," said a voice.

The group spun, everyone with weapons holding them high. They still had just the wooden stakes, the silver stake, and a prop gun with an orange tip they'd found in a shoulder holster beneath a coat two rooms back. It'd probably be useless against vampires, but sometimes vampires had human familiars who were allergic to bullets. Orlo had figured why not and shoved it into his belt.

"Relax, Shadow Stalker. It's us."

It took Orlo a minute, even though the room was brightly lit. Watching, Amelie could tell two things. First, Orlo hadn't forgotten their bloody encounter as much as he pretended; the ghost of that experience was still clinging to him like stubborn fog. Second, he'd lost his enthusiasm for the game. Jason Guerey had used Orlo's in-game name — a name Orlo used in most of his LARPs, not just this one — and yet it'd taken an extra second for Orlo to realize Jason was talking to him. He was thinking as Orlo, not as Shadow Stalker. It was one thing to pretend that all was well, but it was another to feel it. Turns out Amelie wasn't the only one unwilling to let it go.

"You wanna put your weapons down?" Jason went on.

"I don't know. Are you friend, or are you foe?"

"We're all hunters. That makes us friends."

A very bright light went on. Amelie raised her hand to block it and saw that a girl at the rear — one she'd never met, though she knew the rest — had raised it.

"Sorry," the girl said. "I had to be sure none of you had been turned to vampires." She shook the small palm-sized light she'd shone at them, now off. "This is ultraviolet. Bought it from a dealer."

"Where did you find a dealer?"

"Operates out of the general store. Have you been to the general store?"

"No," Orlo said sheepishly. It was obvious: Find a place that sells one thing; they're usually selling all sorts of things under the counter. They had game money, and every hour they played, they gained in-game points. If they hadn't been waylaid by probable death, they'd have visited any merchant they could find by now.

"Wow," said Jason, whose character name Amelie didn't remember. He looked back at his guild. "Hey, do you guys mind if we tell the Minervan Guild the general store password, or would you rather we not help them catch up?"

"It's fine," said a thin girl behind Jason. Amelie thought her name might be June, but he wasn't sure.

"Yea."

"Yea."

"Sure."

"Yea."

"Nay."

Everyone looked at the naysayer. It was the girl with the palm light. "Well, I'm sorry, but we had to figure that password out on our own, so I don't see why we should help them skip past it."

"And who are you?" Orlo asked her.

Jason looked back. "I'm sorry. How rude." He pointed at each of the guild in turn, and Amelie found herself impressed that he remembered all their character names, when she certainly didn't remember all of theirs. "Shadow Stalker, Virgo, Kaspar, Camille, Helmut, Mack, and Lady Elizabeth." Now he indicated the girl who'd spoken. "This is Hippolyta, our new leader."

"Why aren't *you* the leader?" Nora asked.

Hippolyta came forward. "Because they voted it to me. Why do you care?"

"I don't," said Nora. "It's just that Jason was second-in-command before you lost your leader and before you joined." Nora was three inches shorter than Hippolyta and half her diameter. Hippolyta wasn't large by any means, but she still made Nora look like a child.

"You guys ever play War of Daggers?" Jason asked.

"No," said Orlo.

"Hippolyta led a guild in War of Daggers that conquered so much land, they had to reset the map and reallot all the parcels. Otherwise, there was no point in playing."

"If you're that good," said Amelie, "why not give us the password? You're already miles ahead."

"Wouldn't you rather figure it out for yourself? Kind of ruins the experience if someone just gives it to you, doesn't it?"

"It's just one password," said Amelie. "And trust me: There are worse ways to ruin the game."

She was eye to eye with Hippolyta. Unlike Nora, Amelie was tall enough to match her. She looked about 25, not slim but not plump, not tall but not short. She had straight brown hair, a sharp, regal nose, and a ring through one eyebrow.

"Tell you what," Amelie said. "We'll trade you something for it, if that'll make you feel better."

"What do you want to trade?"

"Shadow Stalker has a gun."

"Hey! I want this gun."

"Does it fire silver bullets?"

"I don't know. We'd have to find a weapons master to ask."

"The dealer at the general store is a weapons master."

"Huh," said Amelie. "If only we had the password."

A beat.

"'Plasma,'" said Hippolyta.

"Excuse me?"

"The password is 'plasma.' You'd have figured it out. The grocery list you'll find inside only has three things on it: eggs, milk, and malsap."

"What's malsap?" asked Jaden.

"It's an anagram for plasma," said Amelie, "which I'm guessing the store also sells. Probably doubles as a blood bank, which means half its customers are vampires. They double-deal, don't they? Or they're neutral."

"Neutral," said Hippolyta, nodding. "Very good. See? I knew you'd figure it out."

"What was your name again?"

"Lady Elizabeth Jane Warwick," said Amelie.

They shook hands. "It's good to meet you, Lady Elizabeth. I don't plan to lay down, but if we don't win, good luck to you."

"But not good luck otherwise?"

"Hey," said Hippolyta with a sideways smile, "we did tell you about the decoy."

TWELVE
BACK ON TRACK

After talking to another guild of vampire hunters in character, visiting the store for supplies and a few weapons, and deciphering three more clues, it seemed to Orlo that maybe they were finally putting the morning's unpleasantness behind them. It was quickly 1pm, at which point they broke for lunch — and another good sign came when the guild voted to have lunch in-game. Without the need to break character and hit a real-world food truck, things after lunch were almost normal with the Minervan guild.

Amelie had either given up on trying to reconcile what happened or had been driven to forget it. She re-engaged in the game, allowing herself again to be called Lady Elizabeth while calling others by their character names, not their real names. Jaden perked up quickly as well, shaking off the shadow he'd been carrying since seeing whatever they'd seen, but now didn't have to think about anymore.

The game, too, was going well. They'd already reached the point minimum required for Day Two play, which would happen tomorrow, one floor up, for all qualified guilds. They hit the minimum at barely 3pm, with nearly two hours left. Any points they gained from here on out were gravy, and they'd almost re-gained the lead their earlier gaffe had let Jason's team accumulate.

The casual tip Jason Guerey's team had given them about the decoy car keys turned out to be a lifesaver. They learned later that the keys were to a Mustang owned by a vampire named Molunay. Molunay was between clans, so like many homeless humans, he slept in his car. Difference was, Molunay slept in the trunk, not the back seat, for reasons of coffinlike coziness. If you used the keys to start the car, the vampire heard you and emerged — and then not only killed you whether it was day or night (the car was in an underground garage), but more importantly stole all weapons and supplies in your inventory and, as icing on the cake, cost your team fifty experience points. After re-spawning, those robbed by Molunay were usually incapable of completing the remaining challenges in time (no weapons, no anti-vampire powers) — and unless they already had a huge lead, those folks ended up disqualified for Day Two (and hence Day Three) play. DQ'd players could stay involved as non-player characters, but NPCs weren't eligible for prizes. When he learned this, Rohit announced he'd rather be dead for real than play a waiter in an in-game restaurant.

What's more, the keys were constantly re-set as a trap to trim the number of guilds able to advance. Any team who crossed that random room would find Molunay's keys, those who used them were always able to find the car and fight the vampire ... and Molunay almost always won.

Only after learning this did Orlo realize how big a bullet they'd dodged. The problem was, they hadn't dodged it through skill. They'd survived thanks to a chance encounter with Jason, known here as vampire hunter

Gustavo Reynaldo. That made Orlo feel indebted to Gustavo and Hippolyta's team, so he dragged his own guild off-mission to find them and repay the karma.

There's a vampire nest inside Hotel Desuis, he told them. *If you book there tonight and don't get a room with a window and an exit plan, the Game Master will declare you dead or turned by morning.*

Nora/Camille, watching the game clock, supplies, and probable overnight advantages, hated Orlo/Shadow Stalker a little for warning the competition of the trap. Despite this, their mission of conscience turned out to be yet another boon. Before Shadow Stalker proposed the side quest, Nora had been planning to take them to a known vampire bar just as the sun was setting — but doing so would have been bad. As it turned out, if you went to the bar within 30 game-minutes of sunset (before or after) the vampires there were extremely horny and would lure you into a sex-fest that burned two badly-needed game-hours. Tapping out wouldn't save you, either. Even if a player declined to participate using the safeword, time still came off the clock. Baron Helmut's explanation was that even if you didn't want to have sex with the vampires, it was impossible not to watch.

Nora (not Camille; this was definitely a real-world discussion) explained patiently to Orlo that they didn't owe the rival guild anything for saving them a second time — this time from the sexual time-suck. That had just been good luck. The two guilds were even now, and it was time to get on with the game.

"What now?" asked Virgo Blackheart.

"Ze sex fest," said Baron Helmut.

"We avoided the sex fest," Kaspar Ripley explained.

"Ze *udder* sex fest," said Baron Helmut. "Vut? You sink you can play fampires und not end in ein sex fest?"

It sounded like he was kidding, but Orlo knew he was not. Despite all the organizers' talk of making it possible for less sexual folks to avoid the sexy aspects of vampire hunting, it was starting to look like all of Day One's roads ended in an orgy. Not a literal orgy, of course; the piles of writhing bodies were nominally about biting, drinking blood, turning humans into vampires, and humans grinding on vampires because everyone knew all vampires were irresistible. But they *looked* like orgies. If not for all the pasty skin that would be revealed, they might as well have been naked.

It became a question not of *how* to finish the day, but of *which* vampire sex marathon they should join.

"What about the people who are grossed out?" Amelie asked, stepping out of character.

"Zey lose," said Baron Helmut. "Jus like een life."

Nora seemed to assume a real answer was warranted. "I'm sure you can just walk on through and end the day early with whatever points and inventory you have. I was talking to another hunter back at that town hall thing. He said he gets the impression the orgies are more like a happy hour to end the day. I mean, you'd miss out on some opportunities for extra points, but ..."

Orlo, however, had a better idea.

He'd met someone too — a vampire describing himself as a turncoat. The turncoat had hissed at him from an alley, staying low to avoid the evening sun.

"I know where the leader of the Wentworth nest will be tonight," he told Shadow Stalker, "and I'll tell you where, if one of your guild will let me feed."

Shadow Stalker wanted the advantage without the hassle, especially given the trouble the guild had had in making group decisions today. So while the other six listened to the town hall meeting, he slipped away and, in secret, played human cow himself. The vampire was as good as his word, leaving Shadow Stalker with plenty of vitality points and health to finish the day. In exchange, he gave him the name of a club: The Pretty Kitty — where, if they asked for Bane, they might just come within inches of the most powerful vampire in the game.

And lucky for the guild, Shadow Stalker still carried his silver stake.

Oh yes. There were plenty of points left in the day for the Guild of Minerva.

THIRTEEN
DANCE 'TIL YOU'RE DEAD

The Pretty Kitty was full of bodies, but two things about the crowd were clear from the start — at least to Amelie.

The first was that almost everyone inside was either a volunteer who'd begun the day playing a vampire or a player who'd been turned vampire and was hence out of the game. She knew this because the rules said vampires could smell players while they were still human, yet the vampires at the Pretty Kitty were dancing and laying in pillow-lined piles, not scenting the air for humans.

The second thing she saw was that the few humans who *were* in the place were supposed to be there. They were part of the setup, not vampire hunter player-characters. Vampire hunters had a look, too: They were on a mission, they seemed uneasy and nervous, and they simply *stuck out* — squares in an otherwise cool crowd. If there were other hunter clans here, the vibe would be tainted. The vampires would be defensive, waiting for attack. The hunters would be circulating with weapons, waiting to strike. But none of that was here. There was no aggression. Only the seduction of a rapturous evening in the making.

"Let me see," said Rohit, forgetting to use his Baron Helmut accent. He'd said on the walk around to the Pretty Kitty's hidden entrance that he hoped they'd made things authentic. Vampire orgies didn't pull punches. They orgied 'til the break of dawn. No amount of assuring Rohit that any sexual festivities would be simulated could calm him down. *Maybe they're doing two things at once*, he said. *They could be closing Day One of Vampire Dominion ... and shooting porn at the same time. You never know.*

He peeked in and then moaned, clearly disappointed.

"I don't think there are many humans in there," Nora said as her alter-ego Camille, confirming Amelie's thoughts with a peek. "If we all walk in together, they'll swarm us. I should go first. I'm half vampire, so they won't smell me."

"You want to kill Bane by yourself?" asked Kaspar Ripley.

"If I thought I could, I would," she said. "I don't mind dying, even if they don't let me re-spawn, if it helps the guild. Problem is, I doubt you'd get to keep any points I earn from killing Bane if *I'm* killed ... and I *do* mind dying for nothing at all."

Camille explained the rest of her plan. She'd purchased a salve that imbibed the essence of whatever it touched. According to the weapons master, she should be able to rub it on her own skin, then use it to give the others her own vampire scent — which was to say (since vampires had no scent) to cloak their natural human odor. Kaspar and the Baron, whose long black outfits easily passed for vampire garb, should then be able to circulate without the vampires noticing. The referees inside knew that Shadow Stalker had been fed upon recently by the vampire turncoat, so he'd have some natural protection. Together with Camille, that made four who could lay low, position themselves as needed, and be ready to spring (and then escape) when the time came.

"Okay," said Lady Elizabeth. "So that takes care of you guys. What about me, Mack, and Brody? Even with your magical salve, I doubt we'll pass for vampires."

"You can be slaves," Baron Helmut answered.

It sounded like a joke, but Camille nodded. "Pretty much. Look inside. See those waxy-looking people over there?" She pointed. "They're human, but they're not hunters. They're zombified slaves. Cows, kept for feeding. You need to look the way they look."

Amelie tried a zombified expression.

"More whipped," said Camille, watching her. "More vacant-eyed. Come on, seriously."

"I don't know how to be vacant-eyed," Amelie snapped. "It's not exactly something I've practiced."

"Just like ... really, *really* stupid."

"Also not something I've practiced."

"Hey," said Brody, coming closer. "Remember that dumb kid, Colin, who lived in our dorm?"

"Um ..."

"Pretend you're him."

Amelie tried again. Then she did simple math in her head while pretending to be Colin.

"Excellent," said Camille, watching the transformation.

Shadow Stalker approached Amelie a few minutes later. They all had their disguises in place, and the four could-pass-for-vampires were pairing with slaves, discussing where to go and when.

"Guess you're with me," said Shadow Stalker.

"Into the sex piles," Amelie said, nodding.

That made Orlo uncomfortable. He squirmed, dropping

from character and looking suddenly naked. "Um, yeah," he said.

The small club — perhaps for all its occupants — was stuffy with the feel of bodies. Electronic music filled the air, either spun by an up-front deejay or simply recorded ahead and played back. The lights strobed, causing faces to jump out from the dance floor's shadow, then retreat right back. All movement around Amelie was too-close and alien. The strobe effect made the vampires look like insects: all limbs, jerking in stop-motion from place to place.

A female vampire came alongside them, then slid her hand sensually up Orlo's — Shadow Stalker's — arm.

"Hey. Haven't seen you in the Pretty Kitty before."

"I'm new in town," he said.

She moved closer, now pressing her full body against his side. Amelie was suddenly a third wheel, pushed away for this new aggressive partner. She found herself watching his stern face, wishing he'd say the safeword to end this. They'd still be able to go after Bane, right? It would just keep Amelie from having to watch the girl rub him in the meantime.

"Come," said the vampire. "I want you to meet my friends."

As they'd agreed outside, Shadow Stalker let himself be led. Their plan seemed to be working; the woman was treating him like a vampire, not food. That was the way she kept looking at Amelie, though: like a snack that hasn't realized it's lunchtime.

"Is she yours?" the vampire asked Shadow Stalker.

Obviously she was with him; that wasn't the question. The real question was a deeper one. "She's mine," he answered.

They moved toward a pillow-lined pit off the dance

floor. The lights were dimmer here, strobes flashing between off and moderate instead of moderate and bright. The sounds, owing to the pillows, were a little more muted: a drum played with blankets inside.

Four vampires looked up hungrily at their approach. Two were male and two were female. The most prominent male wore a black leather vest that was wide open, displaying a surprisingly well-muscled chest. He looked at Amelie like a lover while the females went for Shadow Stalker's legs. They twined around them like snakes.

It began to feel like there was nobody else in the room. Amelie's vision tunneled; suddenly she could only see the man in the vest. From somewhere far away, she saw another attempt to enter the scene, but the first man turned, spoke to him, and then he slithered away.

"Lay down with us," he said.

"Lay down with us," all three women echoed, as the one leading Shadow Stalker joined the others. All the vampire women had pushed up, half-exposed cleavage. Maybe it was the room's warmth, but all their breasts were heaving, glistening with a sheen of oil, maybe of sweat. Their hands busied themselves as the group moved to horizontal.

A blip of time passed. It felt almost like falling asleep. Then Amelie was awake again, and the male vampire's hands were on her waist. One moved higher, caressing the lower half of her breasts through Lady Elizabeth's corset.

The safeword formed on her lips, but she decided to let it go a bit longer. They had work to do, and it's not like he was outright fondling her. Yet.

Meanwhile, one of the women had her hand on Shadow Stalker's thigh, moving higher. Another had hands on his chest, her mouth very near his neck. Her head moved like she was scenting him, her nose brushing exposed skin. All three women's movements were liquid: fluid armatures with heavy counterweights.

The man ran his hand up her neck. She saw his face, very close, the tip of his nose brushing her skin. She watched his eyes. Those deep, soulful eyes. She felt her own eyes close. She felt a sigh escape her lips.

"Vampire Dominion," she said. She had more to say, but the words wouldn't come out. Her lips were sluggish. Her eyelids were heavy. *That's enough.*

He didn't move. He didn't advance, but he didn't back off, either.

"Are you sure?" he whispered into her ear. "You could take it back. Nobody heard it but me. Maybe you didn't even say it."

"V—" she said again, but then she shook her head. "No. I didn't say it."

"You are fully here."

"I am fully here."

"You are enjoying this."

"I am enjoying this."

"Touch her," one of the women purred in Shadow Stalker's ear.

By now, emotions were starting to roil and combine inside Amelie. She didn't feel precisely like herself. She heard the facts line up like dominoes: Orlo was beside her, his body pressing hers, and both of them were breathing heavy, slow. Words dripped like honey. The woman went on: "Touch her like you want to touch me."

Orlo looked back at Amelie. His expression threatened to break the moment: He wanted to obey, but knew he shouldn't at the same time.

He heard me, she thought. *He knows I wanted to stop.*

The vampire's hand moved up her leg to her knee,

raising Lady Elizabeth's elaborate garb. A tingling began. An electrifying of nerves, running to her core through a red-hot center.

He knows I don't want to stop anymore.

Reality threatened at the door of her mind. *This was a game. This was all for play.* The fictional clock stood at maybe twenty to midnight, and that meant this charade would only last another five real-world minutes. When that time came, everyone inside would stand up, laugh, shake hands, and go back to being everyday people. The man touching her (the man touching her higher and higher, and for some reason she didn't want him to pause) was just some ordinary joe. Did she really want him to keep going? Did she really want ... But no, she couldn't even think it. It was too strange. Too unlike Upstanding Amelie, who wasn't a prude ... but wasn't whatever-this-was either.

Someone else appeared: A tall, handsome man with dark eyebrows and a narrow, hawklike face.

"Let her go."

The new vampire was talking to the other vampire, not to her or Orlo.

"Don't let me go," Amelie countered. She vaguely remembered something about a mission. About a game.

"If she's your kin ..." said the new vampire.

"Please," said the man touching Amelie. "She's no more my kin than you are. Not in any way that matters."

Were they talking about *her*? They couldn't be. Yet she could only ask questions in a floating haze, bobbing like an buoy in turbulent seas.

"Arek ..." the man said.

"Now *you* touch her," the first vampire told the second.

The man seemed shy. Amelie half sat up, then found his eyes. Without understanding why, she reached for his face and cupped his cheek. She leaned in, but he pushed her away.

"Hey," said Orlo beside her. "You two. That's enough."

The first vampire turned to the second, and it was in that moment that Amelie realized she knew him. She'd seen that face before — maybe both men's faces. Why were they so familiar? She almost knew, but didn't. When she'd approached the pit, it'd been the first man and another, and his face had been turned. Still she'd sensed something from him. Something like danger. Why had she gone forward anyway?

I know you. I saw you. I ...

Knowledge popped into her mind: She knew who he was, all right. The knowing thrilled her, setting her nerves on fire. She closed her eyes and succumbed to a full-body sigh. What she'd realized shouldn't turn her on, but it did.

The vampire's fingers crawled higher and higher. Unlike Lady Elizabeth would have done had she been real, Amelie wasn't wearing six starched petticoats. The way was clear. There was little between him and her.

His hand moved higher, gliding on bare and seldom-stroked skin. Amelie's mouth opened. Her head tipped back in invitation.

"Hey! I said *that's enough!"*

But instead of retreating or answering Orlo directly, the first vampire — the one the other had called Arek — looked him in the eyes. Orlo's features immediately slackened.

"You aren't listening to the ladies," Arek told Orlo. He looked each of the female vampires in the eyes, too, then moved back to Orlo. "They told you to touch her." He rolled back, exposing Amelie. "So touch her,."

Amelie watched, not wanting Orlo to obey ... and very much wanting him to obey at the same time.

This is Orlo. This is ORLO! He's your friend!

But with the vampire's hand so high on her leg, Amelie was losing control. It was going to happen, right here in front of all these people. She was going to pop, and she knew she wouldn't be able to stay quiet when she did. It was a delirious sensation, needful of more.

Now Orlo's hand joined the vampire's. He leaned forward, and his face was not his own. Amelie let her eyes close once more, then tipped her head back for him this time. His lips brushed her skin.

The music's beat slowed.

Then, a commotion. The sensation stopped all at once, retreating like a mouse into its hole. Amelie blinked, seeing Orlo very close, seeing a confused and maybe embarrassed expression on his face, but also seeing

(*How could you?*)

from the eyes of Nora, dressed as Camille Usher, now in the enclave as the plan they'd discussed began to hatch. Nora was looking down at them both, Amelie with her custom dress bunched high and Orlo's hand ... yes, the second hand was right there on her tit, just two layers of fabric between them.

Shouts from the front. Nora's eyes hardened. Then she dove all at once

(*howcouldyouhowcouldyouhowcouldyou!*)

and her hand shot down Orlo's pants. Amelie felt red-hot anger that wasn't her own hand, losing track of everything. The two male vampires looked up at Camille with interest, at Nora with interest, but did not interfere. Only after Nora's hand came away with the silver spike did she understand. *Oh, right. She wasn't reaching for his dick. He'd had the spike in his belt.*

Nora tossed the spike. Virgo Blackheart caught it and

slammed it into the chest of a rather large man wearing false sharp teeth — a very important man that Amelie, in her haze, hadn't even noticed. The big man faked agony, fell over, and then there was an uproar as Nora, Brody, and others she could no longer see ran from the place. And then again: *Oh, right.* She and Shadow Stalker were supposed to run too, now that Bane was dead.

But the light had left the place — or, rather, with a rustle of papery wings, she'd been dragged to a different place. Amelie snapped awake to find herself somewhere new: a corner of the club, hidden from others. The first vampire, Arek, was right in front of her. He was pretending to glamour her ... except that he was succeeding, somehow.

"You want to go willingly," he told her.

Amelie agreed; she did want to go, wherever he wanted to take her. "I know you," she said dreamily, starting to float again. "I killed you, under the stage." There was alarm — perhaps terror — that should have gone with her surety, but suddenly the whole sub-stage scene from earlier felt to Amelie like no big deal.

"If only," Arek said, and smiled. It was the cocksure smile of a high school jock. "Now we wait. Wait for JJ."

"Who's JJ?"

"I am," said a new voice, but it wasn't JJ. Amelie didn't know who JJ was, but this wasn't him; this was Jaden.

Before the vampire could react, Jaden thrust the silver spike into his heart.

Amelie snapped awake again, aware only now that she'd been half asleep. She saw what'd happened with clarity now: The vampire had dragged her from the post-assassination melee, Jaden had seen it, and then Jaden had taken the silver spike from Brody and come to her rescue.

Except Jaden had made a mistake. He should have

guessed these two vampires were real — and yet he'd come after them with an in-game prop.

He'd at least pulled the foam from the spike. The thing cut the vampire just a little, the wound trickling blood. But as the vampire took the spike and laughed, Amelie watched the cut heal. Just as his head, when she'd bashed it, had immediately healed.

The rest of the guild rushed in as Arek began looking at Jaden with incredulity. The second real vampire, JJ, was on their heels. They were in an alcove by the *faux* club's *faux* restroom hallway, now nine people looking from one to the other.

Then Mack, Robert, did something game-brave and real-world-stupid. Amelie couldn't stop him but she couldn't blame him either; for Robert and the others, "real vampires" had long ago stopped being an option.

He leapt at Arek with his cross out and shouted, *"Be gone, foul creature from the depths of Hell!"*

Arek looked from the stake he'd already crumpled like a beer can to Robert with his cross. He gave a scoff that seemed to say, *You've got to be kidding me.* Then he cuffed Robert with the back of his hand: a casual, no-effort motion that sent Robert all the way down the hall to rest against the supply-room door.

Two heartbeats passed ...

One.

Two.

... and as the vampire opened his mouth to hiss, everyone seemed to realize everything at once.

Vampires exist.

Two of them are in front of us right now.

We've got no weapons, they don't mind crucifixes, and shit's about to get real.

"RUN!"

Amelie didn't know who'd shouted, but she complied anyway. She found herself in Arek's grasp, his arm effortlessly holding her back. She batted at him; he seemed only annoyed. Finally he looked her hard in the eyes and said, "STOP." Then when Rohit tried to take advantage, Arek looked at Rohit and said the same thing: "STOP."

Both stopped, but the distraction gave Brody an opening. He came at Arek with the weapons God gave him, either too stupid or too heroic to see the whole thing's futility. He gripped the vampire from behind, working for a headlock. Arek couldn't shake him immediately; Brody was in a spot he couldn't easily reach. He crouched, then, and propelled them both to the ceiling. Brody was smashed between the suspended frame and Arek's back. He grunted, rebounded off Arek on the way down, and rolled to one side, moaning.

Arek stared the others down. He centered on Orlo, fangs bared and horrible.

Arek leapt, but another blur stopped him. It was the other vampire: JJ. They hissed at each other, but their eyes kept darting toward the humans. Amelie didn't try to move. They'd all seen how fast the vampires could move. There was no way, and nowhere, to run.

"I'm older," said Arek.

"I'm stronger," JJ replied.

They engaged, grappled, and then a familiar scene returned with new partners: JJ with Arek in a headlock this time, usurping Brody's place.

JJ squeezed. Arek's words came out in a croak.

"You ... can't ... hurt me."

"Yes I can."

"I ... command you! You must ... do as I say ... through the maker bond!"

JJ blinked. His eyes softened and his arms relaxed a little. Amelie saw it: at the other's command, JJ could do no harm.

Jaden had been throat-chopped in the shuffle. He got to his knees, choking like Arek was choking. Both vampires looked at him.

"Maker bond," he croaked. "That's ... not a thing."

Amelie saw two things after that.

First, JJ snapped to focus and broke the other vampire's neck.

Second, even after everyone else had run off, she remained where she'd been. She kept hearing Arek say *STOP* inside her head. She kept thinking how wrong it would be to run away from him now. How incredibly rude. Nobody from the other side had dragged her off, either. They probably assumed she'd come on her own. But then, why would she do such a thing?

She realized someone was standing beside her. It was Rohit, who'd also been told to stop. He looked like Amelie did: interested in the situation, uninterested in leaving. So they hadn't *all* run off after all. Just the other five ... and, now that she noticed, JJ the Vampire was gone, too.

There was a crack from the floor. Arek stood as his bones knitted, his movements like claymation.

"Fine," he said, taking her wrist in one hand and Rohit's in the other. He looked at Amelie. "You're the one I wanted anyway."

FOURTEEN

VAMPIRE

The vampire was like a hole in the room. He was there, but he wasn't there at all.

Nora, watching him, didn't understand. Her lack of understanding was so deep and so mind-bogglingly compelling that she couldn't delve deeper — couldn't let herself think too long on the most impossible fact she saw before her: that JJ was, in fact, a creature of legend. Everyone knew vampires didn't exist, just like zombies and Santa Claus, but there was no denying what they'd seen. Combining the truth of the game's ending and the truth from this morning, they'd be more insane to doubt than to believe.

What Nora didn't understand wasn't JJ's being a vampire. She *didn't* understand that, but it was too large a thing to focus on now. What caught her more in the moment were more mundane issues — questions of rules and lore. Also, issues of allegiance and who should fear whom. JJ had come with them when they'd fled, and nobody had questioned it. They'd all seen him save their skins.

They'd gone the only place they could think, though who had been leading the group during exodus, Nora couldn't say. They'd gone up a flight of steps, over the bridge connecting convention center to hotel, then up more stairs and all the way to the suite they'd pooled together to rent for the tournament. When they entered, JJ entered. By then everyone had noticed the vampire in their midst, but they noticed retroactively. By the time JJ was truly seen by the guild, he'd already been with them for a while. He'd saved their necks by breaking Arek's. It seemed strange, despite his nature, to think him dangerous.

So they'd neither invited JJ nor disinvited him. He'd gone to the corner and sat on a ledge above the hotel heater, looking out over Detroit.

Watching him (in truth *fascinated* by him; she may have gotten some glamour shrapnel from the pillow pit at The Pretty Kitty), Nora wondered what compelled JJ. He hadn't been invited into the room, so how had he entered? Was the "invitation" thing crap, or were there special rules for hotels? Maybe hotels were public: not real human domiciles. More questions followed: Could JJ see his own reflection in a mirror? Was he vulnerable to silver, holy water, or wood through the heart? He had fangs, but they came and went — retractable like a prop knife. How did *that* work? His skin was pale. His fingers were long and thin: perfect guitar-player's hands.

JJ looked up. Nora hadn't meant to get so close, but here she was anyway, having moved toward him without conscious intention. She looked away when he glanced up, causing brown hair to flop against her face.

"You're wondering if I'll hurt you," he said.

"Can you read my mind?"

"No. But that's what I'd be wondering, if I were you."

He wasn't smiling. She may have made a big mistake.

"What's your name?" he asked.

"Nora."

"Mine is JJ."

"I know. I heard it."

Finally a small smile kissed his lips.

"The answer is no. I don't want to hurt you. *What* I am does not change *who* I am. The reason my kind hunts yours has nothing to do with us having an aggressive nature. It's more that our society makes us so. We are elitists. We believe nature put us on top. So of course we do not tend to see you as worthy of empathy, like ourselves. You are lessers. We are kings."

Despite the tone of his words, Nora came closer. She sat. She was within easy reaching distance even if he only had the speed of a mortal.

"All I know is a lie," he said.

"What do you mean?"

"I am supposed to be a predator. I am not a predator. I am supposed to serve my maker, yet I've never wished to do so. I was taught certain rules — certain things that were meant to be true, and upon which I've built my everyday — and yet I learn more with each passing hour that they may not be as unshakable as I believed."

"I don't understand."

JJ jerked his head toward Jaden. "What's his name?"

"Jaden."

"He knows us."

"You've met?"

"I mean he knows my kind. He knows ..."

"Go ahead," Nora told him. "Say it."

"He knows vampires."

Nora nodded. "He says he's seen them. Seen those like you."

"He likely has. We used to hide in the shadows, but our leader has pushed for more and more exposure. Less and less discretion. For him it is a matter of pride."

"What's it got to do with Jaden?"

"He knew the maker bond was a lie."

"What?"

JJ seemed not to hear. He was shaking his head, his entire body language defeated. "I had no idea. From the very beginning, Arek told me I must obey. He told me I had no choice, that he could compel me to do whatever he wanted even if I didn't want to do it. He made me betray friends for him. He made me kill for him. He made me feed for him."

The words were dipped in blood, almost literally. Nora knew she should be afraid, but wasn't.

"But don't you have to feed anyway?" she asked. "Even if he didn't tell you to?"

"I am the vampire version of a vegetarian. I tasted human blood early-on because Arek told me it was all that would nurture me. I found it not to be true. I considered what you see in movies, where vampires rob a blood bank, but it isn't the hunt I object to; it's the blood itself. It repulses me. But I needed to live, so I turned to animals. When even that began to feel wrong — or, in many cases, disgusting, as with feeding on rats — I eventually stumbled on a solution. I now feed exclusively on blood sold to me by a Kosher butcher. They drain the blood before they prepare the meat, and I am happy to use what they'd otherwise discard."

"But ... You didn't know you could disobey him? How's that possible?"

JJ sighed. "In a sense, vampires are able to communicate without words. It is not telepathy in the way you usually think of it — more like instinct: a knowing without an obvious source. If Arek is hurt, I'll know it even if he's far away. His pain can be as intense as mine — crippling, really. But that ability isn't carried in the mind. It's carried in the blood."

Nora sat, finding she was able, despite the circumstances, to get comfortable.

"We call it 'blood memory,'" JJ continued. "Sometimes more broadly: 'blood ties.' The most powerful among us can look up and down their family trees, sometimes able to recall the memories of vampires four or five generations back as if those memories were their own ... even if the vampire who first lived those memories is gone. But using blood ties is like meditation, and does not always come easy. To some of us, the knowledge it brings is subliminal. Arek is particularly good at manipulating the blood bond between us, and I think now that he implanted a false belief in my mind just after he made me: namely, that I must obey everything he tells me or else suffer pain and death."

"It's not true?"

"It would seem, based on what just happened, that no. It's not true."

"And all it took was Jaden saying so? You just believed him, instead of your maker?"

"It's less that I believed him and more that it gave me reason to question a belief so deep within me, I'd never once considered it might be a lie."

Nora sat with that. Jaden didn't know everything. He'd lit with expectation when Robert pulled out his cross, but that turned out wrong. But even if he'd only guessed, he'd guessed well. The humans in the room owed Jaden their lives. Without that tidbit, JJ wouldn't have known he could break Arek's neck. And if he hadn't, Nora doubted they'd be alive right now.

"Is he dead? Did you kill him?"

"No."

"It takes a stake through the heart."

"Or sunlight. Or silver. I'm sure you know your 'silver stake' was probably aluminum."

"Why did you help us?" The question came out like a sneeze, but once there she couldn't pull it back.

"Because what Arek is doing is wrong. He's always been wrong. If I tell the truth, I don't know now whether I'm happy or sad that we've been sundered. I've lived fifty years under his thumb, doing everything he told me. Now I see I never had to, and I wonder at the damage I've helped him cause. So is this the end of all I've known? Or is it the beginning?"

"It's both."

He looked at her long and hard, and for a minute Nora remembered that he was predator and she was prey. Then he was just a man again, seemingly about her age. But if what he'd just said was true, he was much older.

Robert, Jaden, Orlo, and Brody had seen Nora talking to the vampire and come closer. They said nothing. They weren't going to intrude on their conversation, but they were going to listen.

"Are our friends still alive, do you think?" Nora asked.

"At least the girl is. I can feel anticipation in Arek, and that wouldn't be there if she was dead."

"What's he going to do? Screw her?" Nora turned to see Orlo butting in after all, and for a second she saw him inside her mind, back at the club, hypnotized with his hand halfway up Amelie's dress. There was a flash of anger, and then it dissolved to nothing..

"Doubtful. Arek is older than me, and I think he lived a full vampire life before turning me. Creating me was his way of settling down after sowing wild oats. He'd been young, crazy, and foolish, but now he wanted the closest thing we can have to a child. Since, he has been quite the villain — but almost chaste."

"A chaste vampire?" Jaden asked.

JJ put a hand on his own chest. "And a vegetarian. We have all kinds."

Nora heard Jaden wondering at "vegetarian," then whispered back that she'd explain later.

"He believes your friend is his ancestor: a great-great-something, generations down from himself when he was human," JJ said.

"He wasn't acting like any kind grandfather at the club," said Orlo.

Nora looked around, then realized the juvenile comment she was waiting for would have come from Rohit: *Or he was acting like one very specific kind of grandfather.* But Rohit, like Amelie, wasn't with them anymore.

"Our morals are different from yours," said JJ, "and Arek's are different, yet, from most of us." He looked back at Nora. "If your friend is who he thinks she is, he will use her blood to try and become immortal."

"Aren't you already immortal?"

"*Truly* immortal. He could walk in the sun. You could drop him in molten silver and he'd come out laughing."

"Is that possible?"

"I don't know. He believes it is. But the incantation is tricky, and part of it was obscured in the tome we found.

But his uncertainty is a good thing. It means there's time left before he acts. He will want to be sure and get it right."

"*Is* Amelie who he thinks she is?"

"Is that her name? Amelie?"

Nora nodded.

"Does she have a middle name? Or a nickname?"

Nora looked around at the others. They all shrugged. "I don't know. Why?"

"It's important that we find out. The girl he's seeking is called 'Arcadia.' He must have misheard when one of you called her name. But she might still be. She has red hair, and we believe his descendent would have red hair. Arek's hair was not always light brown. As a child, it was red as a stop sign, he told me. The woman he slept with had red hair. He was able to find two in the chain between, using the internet. Both had red hair. And I have not, as yet, seen others here."

"A lot of people wear wigs at these things," said Nora.

"Don't be so quick to kill the dream," said Robert. "If he decides she's *not* the one he wants, I can't imagine he'll keep her around."

"But that's good," said Nora.

"No," said JJ. "It's not."

The implication made Nora worry for Rohit, but she couldn't think about two dead friends right now.

"I'm sorry," he said.

"It's not your fault." So strange, to be comforting something that should terrify her to her mortal soul.

"It is. I helped. I thought I had no choice, but of course I did. In retrospect it's obvious. But then again, Arek has always hidden our kind's truths from me. He has never let us join a nest. We've always been alone, always. All I know of vampirism came from my maker, and now I wonder how much of it was true. Why keep us away from others, if not to keep me in the dark? I should have known. The very first thing he told me about becoming a vampire turned out to be a lie. I should have known more lies would follow."

"What do you mean?"

JJ turned sideways, bringing his feet down from the shelf and taking his knees from near his chest. Nora knew he hadn't glamoured her because everything still felt grounded, but he still radiated an aura. Both men had been beautiful. Like models, they were.

"In life, I played football. I played hard. I wanted to try for the pros, but after high school and college, I'd taken enough hits that I was worried about taking more. I thought I was being safe, but it turned out the damage was already done. By 25 I had an orthopedist. By 30, I had rheumatoid arthritis so bad, I moved like an old man the first few hours of every day. I got some of that from my father, but football had made it so much worse. We wore less padding back then, and I accumulated a lot of the injuries people began making documentaries about decades later. Life was not easy. I carried on, but there was no light at the end of my tunnel. Would living to ninety be a blessing? For me, it felt more like a curse. If I was crippled at 30, I could only imagine what would happen when old age took its bite.

"I was 32 when I was turned. I had some belief and went searching, feeling reckless but unable to care. Arek found me, but he planned at first only to feed. After he was done, when I was still too weak to move, we talked. He told me about his life, before and after. I begged him to turn me, to take away all that pain and make me new again. So he did. But now I wonder if it was ever my doing. Maybe he always planned to do it, but he wanted it to be my idea ... and, in the end, my fault."

"What do you mean?"

He looked at Brody. "I saw you with a blade."

Brody held up his silver dagger. In the lore of their fantasy games, that dagger had been handed down through generations to Virgo Blackheart, for whom it was a powerful weapon. "Cool, huh?" Brody said. "They won't let me use it in this game."

"Is it real?"

"Well, I mean, I use it still in its sheath. I can snap it in tight and everything so it's safe, but ..." He looked guilty. It sounded like he was explaining it to a referee. He'd had arguments about the blade's safety before.

"Let me see it."

Brody handed JJ the blade. He flinched when their skin touched, and Nora saw him mouth to Orlo: *Cold!*

JJ picked a hotel hand towel from the floor, put it on the desk beside his perch, then pulled an old phone book from the lower shelf to put atop the towel. His hand went on that, fingers splayed. By the time Nora realized what was happening and was preparing to shout, he'd already unsheathed the blade, winced, and amputated his index finger.

The room rushed in, but JJ held his knife hand up to ward them back.

"Watch," he said.

The severed finger crumbled to gray ash. The blood he'd spilled, little by little, did the same. The stump was now healed-over, though, and over the next thirty seconds, they watched his finger regrow until it was exactly as before.

"We heal," he said, holding up the hand. The towel had absorbed some red liquid, but the rest was loose ash. JJ's sacrificial setup looked more like he'd let a cigar burn all the way down than cut off a finger. "Sunlight kills us. Wood penetrating our hearts kills us. Silver weakens us, and if it enters the heart, it kills us as well. Usually separating the spine at the neck will kill a vampire, but the line is softer than you'd think. Breaking a neck, like I did to Arek, sometimes creates a physical separation, but even so broken necks almost always heal. Even traumatic brain injury — like a shotgun to the head — will usually heal in time." He rotated the repaired hand. "Anything less does nothing. A vampire always 'heals' to how he was the day he was turned."

"What's that got to do with what Arek told you?" Nora asked. "How he lied?"

Now JJ held up just the finger he'd severed. He held it close enough for Nora to see.

"Do you see this scar?"

Nora nodded. Then she almost gasped, understanding.

"I got that scar when I was seventeen. I was climbing a fence, and I slipped, and a nail opened my finger all the way to the bone." Once more, he showed the scar. "But if I cut off my finger, the scar grows back. That's true for anything about a vampire's body when he or she is turned. Very recent wounds will heal; that's why turning someone who's about to die can save their life. But anything older than a handful of minutes — my scar, *my arthritis* — was mine forever the day I drank Arek's blood."

He put the hand in his lap, then faced them like a casual teacher. "I still have my arthritis. I still have pain. It diminished some; that much was at least true. A vampire does improve at death, but only where it is possible, or where he is already gifted. My pain moved from eight out of ten to maybe five out of ten, but it did not go away. My joints still grind. They swell, because that's how it was when he turned me."

"So vampires have weaknesses," said Jaden, who looked like he was taking mental notes.

"Relatively speaking. Even with bad legs, I can still outrun you by leaps and bounds. Even with grinding knuckles, I could still snap off your thumb if we wrestled."

Jaden shook his head. "I just assumed vampirism made you perfect."

"We are only perfect if we are made when we're *already* perfect."

"And the imperfect vampires ..."

"There are few imperfect vampires," JJ said. "I'm flawed, but my arthritis is invisible. You'd never know if I didn't tell you. I am still fast — faster than other vampires, even, because I was fast in life. I was agile in life, too, and now I'm one of the best I've seen. But if a vampire is turned when he's smart, he'll grow smarter. If he's turned when he's fit, he will become fitter."

"And if he's fat? If he's ugly?"

"There are no fat vampires. No ugly vampires. Not in Logan's world."

"Who's Logan?" Orlo asked.

"Leader of the Vampire Nation. If you've ever wondered why the modern myth says we're all beautiful and strong and sexy, Logan is the one to thank. Anything less than absolute physical perfection is a weakness to him, and once you have that weakness, it cannot be fixed. Vampires cannot train once they become vampires. They cannot gain or lose weight, grow up or shrink, or do much more than change their hair." He held up his entirely-healed hand. "They cannot even lose their parts. It's for this reason I'm most worried about your other friend. The boy. After using her, Arek may choose to turn the girl. She is 'the right type,' by Arek's definition and the Vampire Council's. There are rules about these things. We're supposed to have approval before making new vampires nowadays, but wanton creation is often over-looked if the vampire in question would have been approved anyway. The girl — Amelie — is attractive enough to pass. I'm afraid your other friend, however, would not pass ... and for that reason, he's in danger if he is not already dead."

"Why wouldn't he pass muster?" Robert sounded offended. "What, because he's not a model or something?"

"Because he is not good enough," JJ said. He looked around, considered stopping, then went on anyway. "I'm sorry. But none of you would be."

"Elitists," Brody snarled.

"I've been called so much worse," said JJ.

Even Nora felt sore at what he'd said and the simple way he was dismissing the insult, but it was hard to stay angry. JJ was with them of his own free will, presumably to help. He seemed so beaten by today's realizations, mired in regret for all he'd done when he'd been brainwashed into believing he had no choice. He'd saved those who were in the room and seemed to want to help save the others. Even if he was in it only to keep his maker from immortality, Nora had a hard time not wanting his assistance.

"How do we stop him?" Nora finally asked. "How do we save Amelie and Rohit?"

"I'll find him. I must track him down while he can still die."

"Okay. So how do we help?"

"You will not help," said JJ. "Instead, you will forget."

"You're going to glamour us?"

"Of course. I won't have more of you on my conscience."

Orlo came forward. "No. Excuse me, but no."

JJ stood. He was taller than Nora thought — taller than Orlo.

Less proudly, Orlo said, "I know we can't stop you if you choose to make us forget."

"Yes we can," said Jaden. "We can just close our eyes and refuse to—"

Orlo stopped him with a gesture. Even if Jaden was right (and he wasn't; Nora was sure he could overpower them and force their eyes open), mentioning it now was precluding any possibility of playing possum in the future.

"So please," said Orlo. "I'm just going to ask, and hope you'll listen. Let me remember."

Murmurs of agreement rippled through the room. Orlo wasn't speaking only for himself.

JJ looked at all the eyes watching him, then said, "Why?"

"You just told us the rules say we're not good enough to join you. That's the will of *Logan*."

JJ waited.

"Let us prove him wrong. And make a goddamn choice *for yourself* this time, rather than doing what the *Vampire Council* tells you."

Again JJ looked at each of them in turn. "You're sure."

Everyone nodded, Nora included.

"Then I suggest you rest. We will find him tomorrow."

"But—"

JJ held up a hand. "There is time. He must be certain. But there's more. I know him well enough not to confront him at night. He is too strong."

"But Rohit—!"

"A chance you must take, if there is any hope to defeat him."

"Okay," said Brody. "But no offense, we sleep in shifts. I'm not catching winks with a vampire in the room."

JJ must have been tired with a full set of daylight hours behind him — the equivalent of staying up all night — because he was already gathering a nest of blankets in which to sleep on the floor.

"There's no need," he told Brody as he settled in.

"Why not?"

"Because if I wanted you dead, you'd already be dead. I could do it right now ..." He cast his gaze around the room. "... and there's nothing you could do to stop me."

Just as JJ was wondering how exactly they would find Arek, Arek came to him.

JJ didn't plan to sleep, despite the nest he'd made. He was exhausted after a long night followed by a sleepless day, but he also didn't trust the humans much more than they trusted him. Despite the futility of it all, Brody had insisted on taking first shift, keeping watch with that useless blade of his. Their play lore said it was silver-infused, but when he'd severed his finger with it, JJ had felt nothing. There was no silver in it, no silver in the room, no decent stakes, certainly no hammers. It would be dark for hours. So how would they stop JJ, if he went on a rampage? But still JJ wasn't sure enough of it to sleep either, because if he was unconscious, stakes and hammers could be improvised.

He *could* die; that much was sure. Dying would actually be fine, given how his afterlife had worked out — but still JJ refused to let it happen until his soul was mended. He'd done so much wrong under Arek's spell, but at least this morning he'd had the luxury of believing he *was* under a spell. Now he knew better: There'd been no spell

— no "must-obey" clause in the maker bond. JJ hadn't been compelled, it seemed. He'd been duped. It was hypnosis conducted from the inside, convincing him for fifty years that he'd had to obey when he very much had not.

All those horrible deeds now sat squarely on JJ's chest. Because of it, he refused to die without saving whichever humans he could — Amelie, Rohit, or unnamed innocent bystanders. JJ wouldn't die without making Arek pay. Without being a hero instead of a villain for a change.

Lying down and thinking, JJ felt a sensation like being grabbed from behind, then sucked downward. He felt his body go limp. He had just enough time to hope the humans didn't choose now to notice and go for him, but it's not like he had a choice of going where this ... this *whatever* ... was taking him.

His feet landed on what looked like black glass. The entire world had turned black — black but somehow claustrophobic, as if there were walls of dark velvet just outside his radius. The light was coming from nowhere in particular. It was a trick of the mind, seeing without shadows.

"That was stupid," said a voice. Said Arek, who JJ now saw walking toward him across that same black glass.

"What is this?" said JJ, looking around.

"It's your mind. Don't you recognize it? It's obvious. There's nothing here."

JJ felt for truth. He found it. This was a mental thing, happening through blood ties. Somehow Arek had reached out and found him, maker to progeny. The bond existed, even if he no longer saw compulsion behind it.

JJ knew he could escape. He wasn't paralyzed. He could force himself to wake, and he could rouse in the humans' hotel room, sitting up and opening his real eyes.

But he wouldn't. He'd stay. He had a mission, and this was its first step. Damn Arek for making it his own.

"It was stupid to turn on me," Arek elaborated. "You made a mistake."

JJ faced his maker without fear. "You lied. I've always been able to disobey you."

Arek nodded. He looked just as he did in life: slim frame, quarterback body, face like a good ol' down-home farm boy. "So what does that tell you, JJ? Seems to me like all we did, you *wanted* to do."

"I didn't want anything to do with it. With anything you made me do."

"Yet you did it. And as it turns out, you did it of your own free will."

JJ let the taunt go. He wouldn't win a semantic argument with Arek and didn't care to try.

"But I am forgiving," Arek told him. "I am love. I will let you return."

"Are you Jesus now?"

"No," said Arek, "but I know someone who knew him."

JJ shook his head. *Was* it his head? No, this was something like a dream. "I won't change my mind."

"Then I'll have to kill you. And I don't want to kill you, JJ."

"Do it, then."

Nothing from Arek. They didn't have bodies here, and nobody could kill anyone. Arek couldn't find JJ in the real world any more than JJ could find him. He might assume JJ and the kids were still in the conference hotel, but unless he wanted to glamour a clerk and end up on the security cameras — something that would draw attention Arek wouldn't want — he'd have to go door to door to figure out which room they held.

"How long have you been planning this?" Arek asked. "Leaving me."

JJ was surprised. "I didn't plan it at all."

"I see. So it's a coincidence? Just a lucky accident that you left me *here*, of all places?"

"What are you talking about?"

"The plaza around the hotel is lit by mercury vapor lamps. It's nothing but vapor for hundreds of yards in all directions."

"And?"

"Most are damaged. If you want to see why that matters, take a walk under the stars. But please. I worry about you. Wear sunscreen."

JJ's eyes popped wide. *Yes.* He'd heard of this sort of thing. Vampires had great incentive to know more about ultraviolet radiation than humans, and as a result knew things like the factoid on display now: that mercury vapor street lamps, if they were even slightly damaged, put out a lot of UV. It was nothing like the sun, but supposedly kids playing in mercury-lit gyms for too long could get sunburns. For vampires, the effect was a thousand times worse.

"You can't leave," JJ said. "In daytime, there's the sun. At night, there's the lamps."

"I can leave."

"But not with the humans, right? You'd have to go too slow if you've got them with you. You can run fast alone and get away, or you can stay with the humans, trapped in the conference center." He was possessed of a strong desire to look out the hotel window, to see that apron of mercury-lit plaza. When he left this limbo, it was the first thing he'd do.

"You can't leave either," said Arek. "If you leave, I'll kill them. I wouldn't normally think that would deter you, but you've lost your spine since this morning."

JJ nodded. What he'd said, if true, meant Arek was still in the building. Their field of search wasn't infinite, which it had felt moments ago. It didn't seem easy yet to locate Arek, and it certainly didn't feel easy to beat him. But it did at least seem possible. The area was defined. Relatively small. And there was nowhere left to go.

"Did you find my mind so you could congratulate me?" JJ asked, knowing it was a taunt.

"Actually," Arek said, "I find both of us in an unusual and interesting situation. If you don't act — if you choose to leave — I will kill them."

"You said that already," JJ told him.

"Yes. But you're unsure whether they're still alive. I'd say they are, and they are, but you won't necessarily believe me. My past is against me in your mind, it seems. So I'll tell you now: I resent this errand. I resent this place. It reeks of the utmost human desperation. *Fantasy.*" He sneered like it was a swear word. "These people's lives are so impossibly small. So I'll promise you this: If you *do* decide to run off, I won't just kill the two I have. I'll kill them all."

"You wouldn't."

"Wait," said Arek, "and see."

JJ waited for Arek to go on. Finally, he did.

"For me, it's like you said: If I leave without Arcadia, I'll lose my prize — and I can't leave *with* her or I'll burn. So we're deadlocked. We're both trapped here until the ritual is done."

It was actually worse than that for Arek. The book said the ritual could only take place on sacred ground, and conference centers weren't sacred. He'd need to find something like a church, ideally Catholic, in which to do it. Until Arek did the ritual, he couldn't leave, and until he left, he couldn't do the ritual. JJ hadn't told the humans that because desperation would make Arek reckless — and a hell of a lot more dangerous for it. But at least it'd buy them time. Until Arek tried, he couldn't know if Amelie was his girl or not. That, at least, would keep her alive.

"So what?" JJ said.

"Neither one of us can win. You see that, don't you? Either way we both lose. Unless ..."

"Unless what?"

"We're kin, JJ. Maybe one last time, we can make a gentleman's agreement, father and son."

"I'm not your son," said JJ.

"Mmm. And yet you are still as bound as I am. I do not want to have to kill you and if you are smart, you will not want to have to kill me. The psychic trauma when a maker-progeny bond breaks by one's own hand is supposed to be nearly impossible to endure. It will be painful for you if I die at all — but so much worse if you're the one who does it."

"What do you propose?" JJ asked.

"Something as simple as it is terrible. I will play you for it."

"Play what?"

"Their game. Their silly little game. You are now on the side of the hunters. I am on the side of the vampires. The body we hid will not be discovered anytime soon, and that means we have time. So tell your new chums to play hard, and to play fair, and in return I will do the same. But I'm warning you, JJ: If you break the rules, I will break them, too. The plastic vampires here are harmless. I, on the other hand, am not."

JJ considered. There was a path to follow with this idea, at least.

"If our team wins," JJ said, "you'll release the two you have, without attempting the elixir?"

"Yes. And if you lose — to their fake vampires, to me, or to any other team — you'll let me go. We can build a way out if you don't interfere. I will go and you will let me make my elixir. When I'm done, I promise to release her, and you promise not to follow me when I escape."

"What will stop either of us from going back on the promise?"

"Something that means a lot to you for some reason," said Arek: *"Our word."*

Yes. That did mean something to JJ. Unfortunately, it meant nothing to Arek. But maybe that was okay. Maybe he had an idea inside an idea.

"Fine," JJ said. "We'll play for it."

Arek seemed a little surprised, but also pleased. He tipped his head in deference and gave a rare smile. "Then I will see you tomorrow," he said. "Ten AM."

The black space vanished, and JJ woke on the hotel room floor.

It was later than he'd figured. Had time passed so quickly? They were all asleep — even Brody, who'd sworn to stay on guard.

My word, JJ thought.

It was all he had left.

SIXTEEN

DAY TWO

The second day of the Vampire Dominion tournament began as well as it could have, for a fantasy game played with real vampires and life-and-death stakes.

They woke with the feeling of a hangover. Orlo, for one, spent his first several post-waking minutes in a still-drunk haze that somehow followed a night in which Orlo hadn't drunk a drop. During the haze, Orlo tried to believe that nothing strange had happened: It'd been a dream, not reality. Any idea to the contrary wasn't just impossible; it was downright absurd. *What, vampires are real?* And: *What, one of them joined our team and is now sleeping balled-up in a corner beneath his costume robes because a sliver of morning light, in the early hours, found its way between the heavy plastic drape of curtain?* They were the kind of thoughts Orlo wanted to punch himself for having, and yet he couldn't deny that they were true. Forget being attacked by bullies wanting his lunch money. Orlo wanted to steal his own, just to make a point.

Things only got worse (and by "worse," Orlo meant "more like a bad joke's punchline") after the vampire woke.

For one, daylight confirmed that he was indeed a real-life vampire. He roused with his fangs descended, then covered his mouth with embarrassment and moved into the hotel bathroom faster than a cartoon effect. When he returned, when he spoke, the fangs were gone. Orlo understood JJ's cues enough not to ask, but Robert, who wasn't great at social cues, asked anyway. JJ explained that vampire fangs descended when a vampire was excited — usually for food, but all kinds of excitement would do. Waking fanged was his version of morning wood.

Watching JJ skirt the tiny bits of sun that came through the blackout drapes darkened the point — for Orlo, at least. Some people avoided bright light in the morning, but the way JJ avoided that entire side of the room spoke of bone-deep aversion: a fear as instinctive as staying back from the edge of a cliff. He moved like a hybrid between human and animal: like them for all appearances, but yet at the same time entirely different. Every movement, however minuscule, struck Orlo as deliberately throttled. Even though JJ walked, talked, rose, and sat at everyday speeds, the effect looked like sped-up footage of someone moving absurdly slow. He was somehow graceful in a way that the guild members weren't, and yet that was one more thing Orlo couldn't have put a finger on. The vampire's fingers manipulated objects with otherworldly dexterity even in the most mundane of motions. Even taking the room keycard and using it looked, in JJ's hands, like practiced ballet.

The final blow (from a surreal, this-has-to-be-a-joke standpoint) came when JJ told them about his dream ... or maybe it'd been a psychic meet-up that Orlo lacked the vocabulary to describe. They had to *play* for Amelie and Rohit's lives? *That* was how they were supposed to get them back — by dressing in costumes, casting playtime spells, and gathering hit points? Orlo was a proud geek — one of the modern kind who said the word with pride. He was a proud LARPer, having defended the hobby to numerous friends and family. *It's just a game,* he said. Somehow adults were allowed to play games, but only if they happened on a board. Dressing up, past eighteen or ideally twelve, was something most people felt was the domain of oddballs.

That was the impression Orlo constantly fought against, and yet now he found himself on the other side. Yesterday morning, he'd have defended their play to all comers — but today, with lives in the balance, the notion of pretending to be vampire hunters felt unbelievably childish. They knew now that such things were real: semi-immortal creatures of the night that drank blood to live, and presumably the humans who chased them with real stakes, real hammers, real silver bullets. The tiny, padded garden stakes on Shadow Stalker's uniform belt were as pathetic as the in-game silver stake. The idea of facing off against Arek as a game-playing fantasy man was mortally embarrassing. If they had to fight real monsters, Orlo wanted to do it as himself. And he wanted real weapons, not the usual silly ones.

But no, that wouldn't do, said JJ. Arek had been explicit about the wager and how it must unfold, going so far as to return in a later "dream" to clarify the rules. Apparently between dreams, Arek had either read the player manual or interviewed his captives. The second time, he elaborated on the first: There were two more days of play, on the second and third floors of the conference center respectively, and both sides would play both days. Arek would glamour Amelie and Rohit so they'd stay wherever he'd hidden them, and meanwhile Arek would return to the field of play like any other player. He'd pretend to be a fake vampire while they pretended to be hunters. If they ran into each other, Arek would not attack as a real vampire; he'd attack like a human playing one. They, in turn, were not to go after Arek with mortal attacks — a good thing, because Orlo doubted they'd be even a tiny bit effective. The rest was lost in detail, but Orlo had theories about how things were likely to go, assuming Arek kept his word. Since vampires couldn't actually *win* Vampire Dominion (all the vampires were volunteers, not competing players), Arek would probably "win" by disproportionately fighting their guild instead of the others, then glamouring the other vampire volunteers to do the same. It gave Orlo a vivid mental picture: that of their guild striving for the finish line sometime tomorrow with every one of the game's vampires on their heels ... while all of the other teams had clear and obvious paths right to the big prize.

"*If* he keeps his word," said Nora, repeating Orlo's words. She turned to JJ. "Will he?"

"That depends," said the vampire.

"On what?"

"On whether cheating will do a better job of getting him what he wants. As things stand right now, I actually believe him. I think he'll play fair because there's really no choice. It's like I told you. Neither of us can leave. He can't leave unless he leaves alone, but that means giving up on his elixir of immortality. If I leave, he'll find a way out, somehow, and be able to make the elixir ... but he's also angry, and he'll want a new companion now that I've left him. That means he'll turn at least one person here, maybe more. He'll feed on a few of them. He'll kill a few of them. Maybe many."

"Why?"

"Because he's Arek. In the war, he called himself Arek the Relentless."

There were details there that Orlo didn't understand, but he understood enough. Arek was angry. Arek was determined to get what he wanted no matter the cost. And Arek, if Orlo read between JJ's lines, was spiteful. He'd take what he wanted, then burn the rest.

So they ate breakfast and prepared. And beginning at the opening chime, they played.

The details of Vampire Dominion's new Arek Expansion Pack were in no way clear, so JJ suggested they just show up at outside the main elevator bank on the convention center's second floor and follow human instructions the way they had yesterday. Arek was not at pre-play orientation, leading Orlo to theorize that maybe he'd recruited other vampires to watch for him. When JJ explained that Arek hated other people (be they mortal or immortal) and had no vampire friends, Orlo theorized that maybe he'd already turned someone new, and *that* was the watcher they couldn't see. Or maybe he'd glamoured humans? JJ said it was possible — even likely.

At the opening bell — 10am real time, but one minute after yesterday's conclusion in game time — they all filed to their places and play resumed. Orlo couldn't stop looking at the people around him, wondering if any of them had real weapons, courtesy of Arek: if any of them might have been glamoured to stab him in the back.

Rohit and Amelie were also absent from orientation. That surprised nobody; it was far more logical for Arek to sneak into the game as JJ planned to, then let loose once inside. Amelie and Rohit were probably not in play either, JJ explained. Amelie, as Arek's potential heir, was far too valuable to risk exposing. Rohit could maybe have been glamoured against them, but that was risky for Arek. Vampires weren't equal in their glamouring ability, and

Arek, who'd always had little use for humanity, wasn't very good at it. If he sent Rohit out as a traitor, he probably wouldn't be hard to turn back. People tended to resist glamour that went hard against their moral code, and even Rohit was loyal to his friends, ridiculous though that friendship was.

The first hour of play was uneventful. The second hour, however, was host to a melee. Despite knowing that *the game is the thing* and that they therefore should have been trying harder than ever to play Vampire Dominion well, Orlo, Robert, Nora, Jaden, Brody, and JJ ended up sneaking around more for clues about Amelie and Rohit's whereabouts (and the doings of Arek above all other in-game vampires) than they should have. The distraction ended up saving them. The largest and most powerful vampire relic so far in the game had appeared in a presentation theater made up to look like a crypt, and every other team but one went after it at the same time in a massive battle royale. The conflict looked bad from an in-game standpoint: the kind of thing that pits teams on the same side against each other, thinning the herd. But even atop that, the crypt turned out to be a trap. A bunch of ancient vampires with special in-game abilities emerged from burial vaults in the middle of it all, to mass-turn as many humans as they could reach.

By the time the Orlo's guild found out about the melee, the action was over and the field of play had been thinned by more than two-thirds. There were only two teams left wholly intact: Orlo's, and a guild of Norwegian exchange students who'd misunderstood the relic announcement, thinking it to be a lead rather than a definite find. The remaining teams were fragmented: two surviving members of one guild here, three surviving members of a different guild there. The fact that their fellows had been *turned* instead of *killed* meant that those players were permanently out of the game. They couldn't re-spawn, because they were already undead.

Now, fighting their own past teammates in addition to the original vampires, victory for the other teams seemed dubious at best. Supposedly even Orlo's biggest competition — Jason's team — was down to only one or two human members. The morning had been a bloodbath.

"But that's good for us, isn't it?" Nora asked.

JJ, right beside her, gave a noncommittal murmur. Maybe it was good, maybe it was bad.

Somehow the two of them had taken leadership from Orlo, though Orlo had no idea how or when exactly it'd happened. They'd begun the day with Orlo at the helm (their default), but at some point Orlo noticed that he wasn't making suggestions and giving orders. JJ gave some, but because he was a guest of the guild, Nora gave others. Orlo wasn't consulted. JJ and Nora also stayed close, nearly arm-in-arm. It was enough to make the others look at one and other and wonder.

"She's glamoured," Orlo told Brody.

Brody laughed. "Just because she never 'glamoured' for you doesn't mean he's controlling her mind now."

Orlo asked what that was supposed to mean. What, was Orlo a tyrant? Did he try to brainwash? Or did this mean something else? He asked Brody, but Brody just chuckled more.

Orlo found Jaden, who understood vampire things.

"He's controlling her, right?" Orlo asked.

"Sure. In the way Amelie controls you."

Orlo didn't know what to make of that, either.

The two remaining hours before lunch were more or less a total loss. Despite searching high and low, they could not find Arek. That wasn't the point, Orlo kept reminding himself — and JJ, who was apparently calling the shots around here now, kept reminding them as well. If the game hadn't changed (and there was no way to know if it had; JJ said they'd need to take Arek at his word until they saw reason not to), then all that mattered was winning this very human competition, irrespective of vampire interference. Orlo had assumed Arek would be in the trenches, fighting back so they wouldn't be able to win — but it was equally likely that he wasn't around at all, and was instead just hiding, waiting until they lost on their own.

No sign of Arek.

No sign of Amelie or Rohit.

They ran across players they'd met before, like a long-bearded collectibles shop owner named Garth who said he'd seen a nest protecting something his group was too small now to investigate. They saw an 18-year-old girl named Cassie, remembered from their fantasy LARPs, who announced that her leg was now dead; a vampire had cursed it and she'd be dragging it until game's end. Orlo didn't know they could do that. Vampire Dominion really was making its own rules.

They ran into and asked for intel from Bella, civil rights attorney and weekend mage. They ran into and interviewed Charles, who sold bonds at his day job. Hippolyta ran past without any teammates, shouting that vampires were attacking from the rear — but when Orlo's guild entered the place she'd indicated, everyone was already fake-dead. They found more people with cursed limbs, and at that point Nora grabbed a notebook from her bag, took them all to a quiet corner, and began making notes. Orlo tried to peek in; JJ nudged him aside. Or rather, JJ moved in, and

Orlo retreated. JJ's skin was so cold, standing beside him was like being in the breeze of too-cold air conditioning.

Nora's sketches, assembled from today's various intel and tidbits she'd intuited herself, formed a rough and some-times-literal triangulation. There was just one conclusion to reach, and it was becoming all the more clear.

"Cursed body parts," she said in a no-bullshit voice, running down a handwritten list. "A nest protecting a relic so valuable it sounds like more than half the vampires in the game, including all the newly turned ones, are protecting it." She drew a rough map. "We ran into other teams — parts of other teams, anyway — here, here, and here." She pointed at each. "Look what's in the middle."

Brody laughed. "Um, no."

It was the theater again. The theater from the ground floor was double-tall, forming a cookie-cutter hole stamped out of the second level's floorplan. They weren't allowed to return to the first floor today any more than they were allowed to climb to the third before tomorrow, but the theater's two-level design put anyone inside just twenty feet or so from where they'd found the body and, ultimately, JJ. It was a superstitious place, now: somewhere none of the guild wanted to go.

"It's not the ground floor," said Nora, again pointing at her map. "You can see the ground floor, but they can't play down there. We'd just be talking about the balcony."

Orlo had understood that. Nora's recitation didn't change his mind about entering the theater again. He was, if anything, more opposed than ever. The theater at least had several entrances and exits. The balcony only had two: one at each end. If they entered and found themselves surrounded, that would be the end.

"Okay. Then we just take pains not to get surrounded," said JJ.

"Easy for you to say," Jaden told him.

"No. Listen. This is a human plan. If you think the second door might be blocked from the inside like a trap, we just enter through both doors at the same time. Half of us go here." Now he touched the map, and watching his finger, Orlo again was struck by his pallor and strange dexterity. "The other half goes here, through the east door."

"But what about—" Robert began.

JJ held that white finger up. "I'm not finished. There are six of us, so three and three. But then we split again at the doors, into one and two. Two enter, one stays at the door to act as a guard. Nothing can come in after us without us knowing. Nothing can surprise us from the inside without us already having backup."

"I don't know ..." Orlo said.

JJ looked right at him. "There's only one person here, other than this group, who knows we're playing a different game. Only one person who will know if we follow all the rules."

"What, you want to cheat?"

"I want to maximize the group's abilities. I happen to be very fast. I also happen to be very convincing. I'm fairly confident that no matter what's inside, as long as it's human, it won't touch you. Not in a sense that will matter to the game."

"But what if Arek's in there?"

"Again, this isn't cheating. This is just me using the special skills I bring to your guild."

Orlo's brow lowered at that. Was JJ mocking them, or was he actually speaking like a guildsman? The latter seemed impossible, but the former didn't sound right either.

"Look," said JJ. "Nora thinks there are vampires in the balcony, protecting a relic. Most of the teams are already shot; only the Norwegian guild is still intact. Any of the singles, pairs, and trios left from defunct teams could still win this game, but they don't strike me as the kind to team up. Does it seem that way to you?"

Orlo shook his head. Competitiveness ran high at these events, enough that even the intelligent tended to be stupid. The broken teams' remaining members could team up for collective benefit, but problems with that strategy would come when time came to claim the prize. Only one guild could win, so two people working together from opposing guilds would ultimately need to turn on each other. Technically one could win and agree to share those winnings with anyone who helped her, but things never seemed to happen that way.

"If that's true, they'll try to go it alone," said JJ. "But *we've* still got six, and one of them is me. We've got a better shot at getting that relic than anyone else — and if I understand your game at all, *that's* what will put us in the lead."

JJ was understating. In Orlo's opinion, their guild winning the relic would decide the game. There were only two complete teams left, and it'd take a complete team to go all the way. They'd have such an enormous lead if they got the relic, it'd be game over. All that'd remain would be for Arek to honor his promise — not a sure bet at all, but at least right per the rules.

But Arek still hadn't shown, and that made Orlo nervous. He should be here. He should be fighting, taunting, licking Amelie's neck and making Orlo hate him. His absence didn't feel like grace. It felt like something hidden, waiting to be seen. A trap, waiting to spring.

They decided to try, despite the unknowns, after lunch break.

At lunch, they broke character and walked the crowd. They made some small conversations, trying to eke out what others knew. Most were friendly but reserved. A few of the singletons, having decided they couldn't win anyway, were helpful. Details of their findings jibed with Nora and JJ's theory.

The guild was excited. Only Orlo had reservations.

"I don't like it," he told Jaden.

"Why?"

"Because they're vampires."

"*Fake* vampires," said Jaden. "And besides, we have JJ on our side. If they try anything, he can just—"

Orlo interrupted. "I'm not talking about the fake vampires. I'm talking about JJ. JJ and his friend."

"But JJ's on our side."

Orlo nodded.

But deep down, he wasn't so sure.

SEVENTEEN
POLITICS, TRAINING, AND DEATH

If Orlo didn't like it, thought Nora, then fuck Orlo.

It was a liberating idea: *Fuck Orlo.* For years now, she'd thought that exact same thing, but with a decidedly more personal meaning. Forget vampire glamour; she'd been under *Orlo's* glamour for what felt like forever, and emerging from beneath it was like finally surfacing for air after too long underwater. If she'd've said it out loud, anyone hearing would have laughed. *Orlo's spell? Orlo's pure animal magnetism?* In terms of magnetism, Orlo's usual charisma wasn't strong enough to attract loose iron filings. He was skinny, nerdy, and ridiculous, his body all elbows and knees. He wasn't in charge of the guild because he was bold and interesting. He was in charge, if anything, because his geekdom was deeper than everyone else's.

Looking at him now, Nora felt the old familiar tingle, stuck through with a newer and much less welcome tingle. She'd seen the way Orlo and Amelie had been practically doing it yesterday, in that vampire pile. *Now* he'd decided to act on his long-held lust? *Now,* just in time to put his dick in charge of all their lives? Amelie wasn't the tragedy here.

Nora wanted to save her, of course, but really Amelie had made her own damn bed. She hadn't needed to get all saucy in that pile, like she had. Amelie, who'd always stood out for her high cheek bones and flawless skin and soulful green eyes, could have kept her distance from the orgy the way Nora had. But no. Everyone desired Amelie; nobody ever desired Nora. So of course, rather than helping the team, Amelie had fallen right in, obeying the throbbing desires of all those men. And when it happened, what had Orlo done? He'd hopped right in bed with her. Shoved his hand up her dress, practically licked a hickey onto her neck.

Well. If Orlo had finally decided to act on his hard-on, good for him. It wasn't a good reason to upend everything they were trying to do, though, or to shift JJ's mission. This wasn't about Amelie, just like it wasn't about Rohit. Nora couldn't help but notice that, by the way: Nobody was talking about Rohit! They had *two* captured friends, not just one — and Rohit, unlike Amelie, hadn't brought it on himself. Rohit had been playing; Amelie had been laying: laying with that other vampire on one side and Orlo on the other. Yet out of that conspiratorial, lusty threesome, everyone somehow only blamed Arek. Where were Orlo and Amelie's parts in this?

You're jealous.

Maybe. But maybe the voice inside Nora now was just plain free. Unrequited affection was terrible. Rebuked affection was even worse. Nora had dropped hints for Orlo — thousands and thousands of hints. Her intentions couldn't have been clearer, yet Orlo was always rude, acting like he didn't see it. Was it possible he hadn't? Could he really be that dense? No, she thought: Orlo knew she liked him. He'd just saved his glances for someone else ... all the while keeping Nora on the hook because to refuse her outright would be to lose her from the guild. So she was a toy. A puppet. Now, doing something that bothered Orlo, Nora might finally be able to break free.

"How do we know he's not still on Arek's side?" Orlo asked Brody as he watched JJ, close enough that Nora was surely meant to overhear. JJ was talking to Jaden; Nora was eating a cafeteria pudding cup more or less alone. Two minutes ago, though, she'd been sitting in the same spot with JJ, laughing, touching his arm. And they were supposed to believe it was a coincidence that *now* Orlo had chosen to question JJ's intentions? *Now*, right after JJ and Nora had been sharing and sitting close? Maybe she wasn't the jealous one. Maybe Orlo had finally wizened up. Maybe now that someone else enjoyed her company, Orlo finally wanted what he could no longer have. Or did he *want* her to suffer? Did it threaten him, that the real brains of the guild was no longer alone?

She got up, gave Orlo a stare, then walked away without waiting to hear Brody's answer.

JJ kept talking to Jaden. Jaden had his own crush on the vampire, though it was an intellectual one. After years of thinking himself crazy and being told as much, his entire life had been vindicated.

Nora looked at the clock. They had five minutes before the bell rang, and the game resumed.

"So people train?" Jaden was asking.

Nora sat at their table, intrigued by the question and what Jaden might mean. JJ looked at her. There was kindness in his eyes. She sat too close, thinking herself forward. JJ would surely object. He'd make distance, so they'd all three be equals. Instead, he patted her leg. His hand was cold, but she'd stopped caring. Every "accidental" brush with JJ's skin electrified her — enough that she felt almost addicted, continually trying to manufacture more. She didn't mind the chill. She'd created a fantasy to explain it: He was a polar bear swimmer, and he'd just emerged from an arctic river after doing something heroic.

"Yes," JJ told Jaden. "The process has become more and more formal. There are even vampire scouts, who go into the human community to recruit. They find humans who seem like they'd make good candidates, then tell them the truth. The scouts explain our world. They tell eligible humans that they're candidates to join, but they must train so as to fully optimize before being turned, seeing as they'll be locked that way forever. Then ..."

"And people just believe them?" Jaden asked.

JJ looked at Nora again. He turned back to answer Jaden.

"They do more than speak."

"And then what?" Jaden asked. "What's 'vampire training' like?"

JJ's face twisted. "It's ... disturbing."

"Why is it disturbing?" Nora asked.

"What we have used to be seen as a curse. It's not that way anymore. Modern vampires treat it like a gift. I think it's the movies. Your culture has glamorized vampires, but you've also glamorized superpowers — anything that makes a person bigger, better, faster, stronger. People see only what's shiny, and miss what's dark."

"What do you mean?"

JJ shifted as if to settle in, and Nora got the distinct impression this was a topic he'd pondered often, with disappointing conclusions.

"My mother is very old," JJ said. "Soon, she will die. She will probably be sick for a while first; that seems to be the way of things. I'll have to watch it happen from afar. I won't even be able to visit."

"Why not?"

"My family and friends believe I'm dead. They have to. My little sister is now an old woman. I could let her remember me, but the shock each time she comes out of glamour is slowly breaking her mind. My mother wouldn't remember me at all, probably. That's the thing people forget about near-immortality: You can't take anyone with you. You end up alone, watching everyone you ever loved die one by one."

"Couldn't you turn them?"

JJ shook his head. "Mother drifts in and out. She would be an unpredictable vampire if she was turned now. Same for my sister. Besides, the Council would never let it happen. More and more, they control those who enter and exit our ranks. One reason for the training programs, for humans who wish to be turned, is so the Council can license and register them."

"You make it sound like government. Like it's political."

JJ nodded. "You would not believe the politics. We used to be proud. Now we are legislative. Our leadership, at least in America, is fascist."

"Just in America?"

"Europe maintains the old ways. I have met their Council Leader. His name is Karl Stamm. Karl is Gary Oldman's Dracula. Our Logan is ..." He sighed, thinking. Then he finished: "... a politician with questionable motives. Logan wants to expand our ranks because we are so outnumbered — but if it were up to Logan, the entire planet would be vampire. We would live in the open beneath enormous sun-blocking domes. We would keep humans the way humans keep cows, and milk them for blood." JJ saw their faces, then laughed to break the tension. "Don't worry. There are many more moderate vampires in the Vampire Nation, including on the Council. He won't get his way."

Nora sensed an unspoken "unless" lurking at the end of JJ's sentence. Before she could analyze it, though, Jaden spoke again.

"But he's still training."

"That's more about elitism than power," said JJ. "I was not a licensed creation. Arek made me without consulting the Council. It was early, though, before things became as they are now, so it was not hard to win favor being the way I am."

"What do you mean, 'The way you are'?" Jaden asked.

"I look strong. I look able-bodied. I'm in pain all the time, but unless I give in to the pain, it does not affect my speed and power. Forgive my immodesty, but I was considered attractive at the time. All was in my favor. They approved me right away."

"Attractiveness matters?" Jaden asked.

"More and more. Haven't you ever noticed that your culture views vampires as unfailingly beautiful and sexy? It was not always that way. In my day, people still thought of Nosferatu. Do you know Nosferatu?"

Nora and Jaden nodded. Nosferatu, in his film, had been the opposite of sexy.

"You imagine vampires as thin and muscular and elegant and beautiful because we are all those things under Logan. He is proud. He feels we should only be the very best. Even if I wanted to turn my mother and sister — even if it would heal them, which it would not; they'd be stuck as old and feeble for eternity — the Council would never allow it. I'd have to hide them. Forever."

"What happens to vampires made without Council

approval?" Nora asked. "The ones who *don't* train to get maximally strong and fast and ... I guess *ripped* before being turned so they can stay that way forever?"

"They are given a trial. Those who are strong and fast and attractive — those who fit Logan's definition of a 'proper vampire' pass and are allowed to live as official Vampire Nation citizens. Those who are not — the old, the sloppy, the handicapped, those who are strange or obese or too slim — are executed."

Nora could have stopped there, but Jaden was curious: "How?"

"They are chained up inside a chamber in daylight hours. Then the roof of the chamber is opened. It's something of a spectacle. From the shadows, the Council and invited guests watch it happen."

"Where? I mean ..." Jaden looked like he knew he was pushing too far, but didn't seem willing to stop unless JJ stopped him. "Where's your 'Vampire Council' hidden?"

JJ hesitated.

"It's okay," Jaden said. "I shouldn't have asked."

"No, no," JJ said, eager to show he'd given up all loyalty to the Vampire Nation. "It's that I don't know. Nobody does, not even the Council. Logan is terrified of assassination, since that's how *he* gained *his* power, and that terror has made him paranoid. The Council is always moving, its location handled by an algorithm that nobody — not even Logan — can predict or control. It's ... complicated."

Nora, despite herself, felt her curiosity piqued. If vampires existed, she'd assumed they'd live in abandoned basements and under bridges, launching attacks like jackals in the night. The picture JJ painted, however, was of a highly organized organization somewhere between a shadow government and an army.

The lights flashed on and off. It meant they had one minute left. She wanted to know more, but this wasn't the time.

"We should get ready," Nora said.

A minute later, a chime rang. Orlo appeared at Nora's side, but this time unlike most times, she had no strong feelings about his proximity at all. With JJ on her other side, Orlo wasn't intoxicating. Not a whit.

"For better or for worse," Orlo said, eyeing the first set of balcony doors, "here we go."

Brody was frightened enough to shit apple cores. It was an acutely uncomfortable sensation.

Usually, Brody was cool and calm: much more so than his teammates — or, really, most of the LARPers he'd met. Brody had a foot in both worlds: the nerds, but also the cool. At heart his was much, much more of the former, but he'd actually played a sport, had friends on multiple teams, and his last two years of high school he'd gotten nominations and a handful of votes for Homecoming King. Those nominations and votes were mostly a joke (his buddy Ging did it to be an asshole), but it was still far more than the likes of Orlo and Robert and Jaden could say.

But today Brody wasn't cool and he wasn't calm. It had been a rough weekend. Yesterday he'd seen evidence of a murder, watched another in progress, then had decided both were hoaxes and argued hard with his friends, then had been whiplashed back to center with the realization that *Yes, Virginia, there really are vampires and they really are eating the fuck out of people all around you.* Last night he'd slept across from a bloodsucker, his sleep thin and inadequate thanks to stress. Now he was logy and amped-up at the same time. The combination should have brought him to neutral, but it didn't. It was like running a car's heater and air conditioning at the same time: both on maximum somehow didn't make for normal.

JJ was running things. Orlo clearly didn't like it, but Nora was behind JJ as a second, and given the situation it was Nora, their strategist, who should have been in charge anyway.

JJ pointed. "Robert, Brody, and Jaden. You take the far entrance to the balcony. Nora, Orlo, and I will take this one." He repeated the high points of what they'd discussed, but most of that was common sense: flank large groups and keep your distance, use crosses to keep them at bay (since they were presumably playing by game vampire rules), watch the corners and watch your back ... things like that. Brody asked again what would happen if Arek was there, if he decided to play for real. Nobody had been able to answer that, so JJ's response — then and now — was, "If that happens, I'll handle it."

The feeling of shitting apple cores did not go away as Brody followed the hallway around to the second balcony entrance. He wasn't scared of fake battle; fake battle was a safe adrenaline hit with no real danger. What scared him was this sense of blossoming unknown. No matter what JJ said about gameplay being the only escape for both vampires, Brody had his doubts. People could be backstabbing jerks — but vampires, depending on your belief system, were at least in the neighborhood of actual evil. Opening the balcony door might be like opening an engine compartment on a running machine with deadly parts. And to think: He was about to pop the top, then stick his whole self inside.

Brody had his fingers on the door handle when someone behind him said, "Don't."

Brody spun with a prop stake held high. He wielded it like a dagger — as if he meant to do deadly battle with foam on the end.

"It's us," said Jason Guerey. He was with his guild leader, the new girl. Hippo something. He looked at the door and repeated, "Don't go in there."

"Why?"

"It's been charmed. The vampires moved whatever they were guarding. Going in there now puts you into some sort of a vampire spell. Takes off like twenty points."

Brody still had his hand on the door. "We have three people at the other entrance."

The girl looked at Jason. "Go," she said.

Jason ran off, presumably to warn the other group. She looked at Brody.

"Virgo, right?"

Well, no. Brody had probably never been less "Virgo" in his life, despite Virgo Blackheart's gear and clothing. But it was too complicated and ridiculous to explain why this wasn't fantasy for him anymore, so Brody just nodded.

"Mack," she said to Robert. "And ...?"

"Kaspar."

"Close. I was thinking Casper. Like the ghost. No offense."

"None taken," said Jaden.

"Hippolyta," said the girl — maybe because she knew Brody had forgotten, or maybe just to be nice.

"Why are you helping us?"

"Because there's just the two of us now. I was wondering if you'd want an allegiance."

Brody considered. He wasn't in charge of this group. Right now, that dubious honor probably went to Orlo or Nora or maybe even JJ — who, come to think of it, would also be hard to explain.

"Orlo didn't think anyone would want to ally," he said.

"I'm a little more practical than most people. I know we can't win it with just two members." She looked at their three as if just noticing them. "Where's the rest of your guild? You said you had *three* at the other door? Did you lose one?"

"Two, actually."

"Really? I heard Minerva and Nova were the only two guilds that didn't get caught in that big fight. I though you had everyone."

"It was recent."

"Then how do you have six, if you stated with seven and lost two?

Brody thought fast, hoping the other group wasn't about to contradict him to Jason. "We picked up a single," he said.

"So you *do* want allies."

"I should let Orlo decide." He corrected himself. "I mean Shadow Stalker."

"But you just said you allied with a single from another team."

"I ... That's different."

"How?"

"Orlo can explain."

Hippolyta was staring at him. How could the simple logic of this situation require another mind?

The other group came around the bend. It seemed Jason got to them before they, too, rushed in. Hippolyta took the lead, catching everyone up. JJ's presence was left ambiguous: "from another team whose name I don't remember." JJ didn't offer the name either.

When she brought up the issue of allying again, Brody interrupted Orlo's answer and pulled him to the side. Something had just occurred to him, and it looked like Orlo had been about to say yes.

"We can't ally with them," Brody said.

"Why?"

"JJ. How are we going to explain JJ?"

"I already did. He's from another team."

"And he'll just play like any other character, huh?"

Now it sunk in for Orlo, too. The chances that JJ would act like a human had been dwindling all day. Now they were practically relying on 1) his speed and guile and 2) his ability to glamour any humans who saw him into forgetfulness.

"Well," Orlo said, "I guess he can just glamour them, too."

Brody shook his head. "No way. We run into Jason's guild at almost every event we attend. If there's any flaw in our cover story at all, it's gonna come back and bite us. It's okay with the volunteers; they won't know us from Adam and chances are we'll never see them again. But I'm reluctant to shit so close to where we eat."

Orlo nodded. "Okay. You're right."

So they separated. Hippolyta seemed offended and kept looking at JJ as if to say, *Why him but not us?* Orlo told her it was just a matter of convenience, then made up some other stuff that didn't make a whit of sense. At first Brody figured it didn't matter; as long as they left, the job was done good enough. But even when they left, both of the others kept eyeing the group. It was a deeply suspicious look, and Brody worried that what had just happened, too, might come back to bite them.

"So they'll try to beat us to the win," said Nora. "So what? They were going to do that anyway."

Still uneasy, still thinking of the angry and confused and suspicious looks the other guild members had given them, Brody fell back into line. They couldn't storm the balcony after all, so they moved through the floor, trying to get the lay of the day's land. The playing field was different than yesterday, and more than once Brody had suggested going back to this place or that place — but of course those places were on Floor One, and they were limited to Floor Two today.

They had no leads. Brody wished they'd strung the other team along for a bit longer before dismissing them just to get some ideas, but now that ship had sailed. They ended up wandering aimlessly, then stopping with about a half hour's worth of real-world time (two hours of gametime) remaining. The in-game vampires were out in full force now that it was game-dark, meaning they'd lost their daytime advantage. And still they'd found nothing at all.

"Look," said Jaden, peeling back a taped-down shade over an outside window. "It's almost real-dark. I guess it's not only the game vampires that'll come out to play."

Nora stood up. "I think I've decided."

They all looked. Nora was their strategist. Since JJ had no ideas (Arek still hadn't shown, and this was a human game he'd never played) the group decided they'd do whatever Nora felt was best, no matter what it was.

"We go back to the balcony," she said.

Muttering erupted. Nora calmed them with an air-pat of both hands.

"No. Listen. I don't think the others were lying. I do

think there was some sort of a spell put over the balcony. But we've been wandering around for over two hours now and we've seen no clues at all, and no teams that seem to be making headway. The only place we haven't looked is the balcony. I say we *zig* there while everyone else is *zagging* all over the place."

"We'll lose tons of points," said Orlo.

"Yeah, we might, but we're also the only team here who has a goal beyond the game. Everyone's avoiding the balcony, but think about it: We're supposedly playing against Arek, and Arek can take the game wherever he wants if he can control human minds. He'd want to face us and only us, right? So maybe he put himself where no other teams would dare go, and where we'll be weakened if *we* go. But get this: That relic has to be somewhere, and it has to be in vampire hands based on what we know of it. I haven't seen many game vampires at all today. The whole game is lame as hell."

That was true. Playing Monopoly would have been more riveting. Brody had heard many people complaining.

"So what if he took all the game vampires to the balcony?" Nora went on. "And so what if there's a spell? Maybe we'll lose points if we go through it, but the relic *gains* us points. If we don't do anything at all, *nobody's* going to advance to Day Three. Nobody. They'll just declare it a wash, and whoever's in the point-lead will win. And guys? That's not us."

It was the other intact team: the Norwegian team called Nova. Damn them.

"So here's our choices. We do nothing and lose, or we try the balcony. If I'm wrong, we'll lose worse than we already are, but who cares? Losing is losing. If I'm right, though, and we get the relic ..."

Nods were going around.

"All right," said Orlo. "How much time do we have? Real-world time."

Brody looked at his watch. "Twenty-two minutes."

At the same time, Jaden said, "Maybe twenty minutes."

But Jaden was still looking out the window, talking about sunset.

NINETEEN

WHAT WAS HIDDEN

They lined up as they'd originally planned, now with a full day's baggage dragging them down.

With her hand on the same door handle as before, Nora felt trepidation she hadn't felt during her little speech. The logic she'd given her guildmates was right; it was more likely than anything else that the vampires had been in this room all along. Inside, whatever they'd hidden would be safe. You'd have to be crazy to keep going after taking a twenty-point hit — or more than that, because they'd learned since that the spell grew worse the longer you stayed inside the room. That made Nora sure that the relic (and maybe Arek) was inside. Arek wouldn't care about ruining the LARP for everyone else. He only wanted to win.

But that was the other edge of the sword: the thing that made Nora uneasy. She'd said that Arek *might* be inside, but she actually felt his presence was probable. She was sure he'd be waiting, ready for an ambush. For all JJ's talk of needing to fight fair, Nora wasn't sure she bought it. Ambushes were meant to kill people. It meant they might be about to walk right into a Cuisinart.

That was the problem with being so left-brained and organized: you were seldom bamboozled by promises and hope. Logic always won, and logic right now said that if she was in Arek's shoes, Nora would be sharpening her teeth right about now.

Brody, in the second group, had a watch. Nora had a small clock clipped in her costume pocket, and she was looking at it now.

"Five seconds," she said.

Four.

Three.

Two.

One.

It was Orlo who opened the door, and he did so at just shy of a kick. Nora and JJ rushed into the theater balcony, and from the corner of her eye Nora saw Brody and Jaden do the same. In her own group, Orlo remained at the door as guard. In the other group, Robert took the honor.

But the balcony, like the theater below, was dark. It was also too quiet — the padded balcony seats, maybe, absorbing all the echoes.

They walked the aisles for several long minutes, seeing nothing. The balcony was steep, and Nora kept expecting to be surprised from behind. They didn't really have weapons, though last night they'd run to Home Depot for real wooden stakes, which they'd sharpened and smuggled in. The wood's presence was reassuring, but only a little. Nora, for one, doubted she had the strength to stab someone through skin, muscle, and ribs to reach the blackest of hearts.

Her eyes slowly adjusted. Someone had disabled the emergency lights on the balcony, but something lightly glowing below — maybe a still-functional Exit sign — gave an edge to the railing dividing floor from open air.

Someone brushed her. Nora jumped, but it was only Jaden.

"I can't see shit," he whispered. They'd told Orlo and Robert to close the balcony doors, lest something slip out unseen.

"There's no emergency lights. Did you notice?"

Jaden looked around. Watching, Nora could only see the slightest bit of profile. "I do now."

Understanding passed between them. There'd be no reason to disable lights if nobody was up here hiding. They were all alone. There was a camera in the hallway. The Game Master and staff had seen them go in on the cameras and surely already deducted points, but nobody was watching inside.

"You came," said a voice.

Nora startled, jumping about a foot. They all had flashlights, but they weren't supposed to turn them on unless they found something. Nora trained hers on the voice and saw Amelie two rows down — in the last row before the railing. Her eyes were glazed and she was perfectly still, still wearing yesterday's clothes. Twin puncture wounds were on her neck, dried blood beneath them.

"Amelie!"

"You shouldn't have come," she said.

Amelie stepped onto the ledge, the thick brass railing between her feet. A breeze from the air conditioner stirred her hair as she raised her arms. The effect made it look like she was already falling.

"I'm spent. I'm gone," she said in a ghost's voice.

"Get down from there!" Jaden hissed.

But JJ had heard and seen the commotion. He was next

to the others in a blip, with Brody hustling toward them. He was more subtle than Jaden, outright yelling for Amelie to step down — for Amelie not to jump. The commotion made Nora look toward the first door, where Orlo was on guard. He should hear this. And yes, they *both* should hear it (Robert too), but this was Orlo's great love. His time to be the hero.

But nothing. Instead, she saw a shape move inside, past the hair's breadth of light coming from around the door through which Orlo had not yet come.

"Shit," said Brody seeing it.

"Amelie?" Jaden was moving closer. "Amelie, look at me. It's Jaden. You remember me?"

Glamoured. She wasn't herself. Her feet tittered, threatening to fall.

"Guys," said Brody.

But Nora was already looking. There were several shapes in the dark, not just one. *You saw this coming,* Nora told herself.

"JJ," she said.

"I know."

"You need to ..."

"I remember."

He was gone. They'd discussed this. *You will want to fight, but don't fight. If it's a trap, here's what has to happen.*

The lights came on as JJ, all the way down on the ground floor, flipped the breaker. A millisecond later he was pulling Amelie from her perch, rushing her toward the back, shoving her toward the door. It happened so fast, Nora couldn't follow. One second they were in the dark, talking Amelie down. The next they were awash in light. Amelie was gone from before them, but there were at least a half-dozen play vampires creeping slowly toward them, visible in new illumination.

Except they weren't play vampires. Not anymore.

"Double shit," said Brody. He seemed paralyzed.

They came on all at once. Nora reached for the first of her wooden stakes, but then something impossibly strong wrapped her and pulled her back like a bungee. She felt hands. The smell of rotten meat wafted across her neck and invaded her nostrils.

"Clever girl," came a cold voice. Arek's voice.

Nora fought, but Arek only laughed. "It's not her. I tasted her, and she's not my Arcadia." Another titter. "Maybe it's you."

"My name is Nora!"

"Then maybe you're just a snack."

Arek's skin was cold, but somehow his breath remained hot. She felt more than saw his mouth descend toward her neck from one side. She felt the brush of his sharp canines and struggled, but then two things happened: She managed to kick a leg up, hard, right into his testicles. Seemed vampires still had them, and they still hurt. The second thing came right after — and good thing it did, because smashing Arek's balls had done little more than make him mad. JJ came screaming toward them like a blur, throwing Arek ten feet back into plaster. He didn't let go of Nora, though; she whipped after him, still held at the wrist, like a rag doll.

"JJ!"

JJ looked back toward the balcony and growled, then ran toward the summons. Nora remained hooked, unable to flee. Arek extricated himself from the wall, then looked at her like it was her fault. Nora's attention, however, was on the balcony floor. Somehow Arek had turned five or six of the volunteer vampires into real ones, and now they were running around the humans like sacrifices in the making. One guarded each door (were Orlo and Robert safe outside, or had they been attacked, too?) and three or four blurs joined JJ's in the seats. Amelie was staggering toward the rear, seeming to come out of the spell she'd been under. Nobody was paying her any attention; though. All attention was saved for the fight.

"He's not fast enough to take them all," said Arek, laughing in Nora's ear. "But we can watch."

Nora wanted to snarl something at him (*"You're just going to let your cronies do your dirty work?"* would do), but she found herself unable to speak. She could only do as Arek said: only watch, nothing more.

One of the new vampires was creeping up on Jaden, who'd been left gaping when Nora was snatched away. A blur passed him, and only when the blur was gone did Nora see the new vampire burning. It wasn't a fire burn, like a campfire. This was something hotter: a white-hot fire that burned from the inside.

"JJ just killed that poor volunteer," laughed Arek. "And to think — he just came here to play pretend!"

But what else was JJ supposed to do? Nora didn't understand all the rules, but she'd chatted enough with JJ to have an idea. Becoming a vampire didn't turn you evil. In personality, JJ said it tended not to change you at all. But he also said that vampires couldn't be glamoured. Was this a loophole? Could Arek have glamoured humans into doing his bidding, then turned them while they were still his slaves? JJ said it took time to transition from fully human into fully vampire — a period in which, like her own character Camille, the afflicted still carried human blood and could walk in the sun. Had Arek exploited that weakness to make vampire slaves?

Another blur. Another burn. And another. There were, she counted now, just three vampires remaining, excluding JJ and Arek. But they must have locked the doors; Nora could hear fists pounding them from the other side and shouts at the top of human lungs. The three who remained were advancing, crowding Jaden, Brody, and now Amelie to the balcony edge.

"Nowhere to go," said Arek. He'd locked Nora back in his rear-side embrace, his stinking mouth again just inches from her ear. "Nowhere to—"

Something slapped against the balcony railing from below — from the theater side, not where the seats looked out. It was ...

Could it really be a *ladder?*

Something shot up the ladder too quickly to see. Only when it stopped could Nora see its form.

It was Rohit. And he was a vampire.

"Now," said Arek. "Watch."

The three humans didn't seem to know what to do. Nothing made sense. Where had Rohit gotten a ladder? And why had he used it? Couldn't vampires jump? Or was he too new — too powerless yet?

Arek didn't react. He seemed a bit surprised by the ladder, but not by Rohit. He wasn't moving to intervene, meaning Rohit was probably as glamoured as the rest.

Rohit clawed his hands. He hissed. He advanced while the humans shouted his name, to no avail.

He ran at Brody, but then Brody did something rather surprising: He hit Rohit impossibly hard in the face.

Rohit went down, either surprised by Brody's aggression or still human enough to be humbled. He tumbled backward over a seat and sideways into an aisle.

JJ was on him in a second. Nora struggled. She didn't want to see JJ kill her friend.

But then JJ was up, surprising another of the new vampires and — with a twist and a flourish, pulled off its head. The other two scampered away, moving in blurs.

They stood side-by-side with Rohit, seeming to decide there was safety in numbers. They were wrong, though; whatever JJ said to Rohit had broken his glamour. Arek was apparently shit at glamouring, while JJ had chops.

With no weapons and probably without knowing his limits so early, Rohit did all he could: he grabbed the vampire next to him, pushed it to the ground, and began to rip through its neck with his teeth. The other vampire came forward to stop Rohit, but that's when JJ intervened. He must have ripped a stake from someone's belt too quickly to be seen, because a second later the other was burning like a welding torch.

The new one burned beneath Rohit. Apparently he'd managed to separate the head.

Another came from the shadows — one that must have been hiding, maybe as a contingency. This one was faster; it leapt rows of seats in one, then had Brody by the throat. The vampire reared back, fangs bared, and Nora heard herself scream. But before the vampire struck, something appeared embedded in its neck: an arrow, shot by someone climbing the ladder.

It was Hippolyta, who seemed to have bought a new weapon from a weapons master.

She leapt to the balcony, and in that instant Nora understood it all: The girl really had been suspicious; she really hadn't let it go. She'd probably been following them and watching around corners, eager to pursue the leading team that wouldn't let her join. Jason came up the ladder behind her, holding a simple spike — apparently he, unlike her, hadn't had points enough to buy a weapon. If the two of them had been watching, they'd know the truth if they'd let themselves believe. JJ hadn't just been talking about all things vampire for eavesdroppers to hear; he'd been acting like one, too. Their pursuers must have faced a choice: believe in vampires or think themselves crazy. To their credit — versus the disbeliefs their guild had held for so long — they'd chosen the former.

And Rohit? Who knew. Maybe he'd been down there all along, and the ladder was his opportunity.

The speared vampire grabbed the arrow by the shank and pulled. It glared at Jason, who was closer, and charged. The girl tackled him — stupid, but it did at least save Jason from the charge. The creature whipped her off, then stood and fumbled with her bow, which the fall had broken.

While she tried to nock an arrow anyway, the vampire advanced.

"Arcadia! Look out!"

Arcadia.

There was no hesitation. Nora was chattel now, barely more than luggage. Arek flew across the room in a blink with Nora still by the arm, careless if he pulled it from its socket. The wrenching pain was intense. Nora thought she heard something tear, felt tissue part beneath her skin. But she was whole when she slammed across a seat — whole when Arek, far more powerful than his newly-created progeny, easily cuffed the newcomers aside and took Hippolyta, whose real name was apparently Arcadia, using his other hand.

JJ flinched forward. With no hands left, Arek growled

and put a foot in Rohit's back, kicking him at JJ. Rohit flew, his back bent so far he could have touched his heels from behind. The crack that came with it was sickening. He collapsed like scarecrow with its stake broken.

The last new vampire joined the fray, avoiding the humans at last and turning to JJ. JJ raised Rohit like a human shield, then moved close and punched hard around his body. His fist struck the vampire in the chest — *through* the chest — and then the last one was burning. It took Nora a moment to understand why, but then she remembered the ring JJ wore. It looked like wood. Apparently, it was.

JJ was still holding Rohit's corpse. He dropped it, then faced Arek. Arek was outgunned now: Even if JJ wasn't normally his match, he should be now, given that both of Arek's hands were holding women: Nora on one side, Arcadia/Hippolyta on the other.

"Let them go," JJ said. "There's nowhere for you to run."

But Arek just snarled like a beast, bared his teeth, and practically flew.

Nora knew he wasn't going as fast as he could, or being as careless as he could be. She'd seen JJ zip across a room in a blink, but Arek was just running very quickly, taking leaps and crashing through obstructions when he met them. He was protecting Arcadia, Nora knew, but that was okay. If he wanted to protect Arcadia, the same precautions would protect Nora as well.

Down over the balcony railing. Through the lower-level theater doors, which were as locked as they'd been yesterday. He broke through as if they were made of balsa. He stopped to look at a clock, then laughed and rushed for the convention center's front door.

"You can't leave," Nora croaked, finding herself a bit more injured than she'd hoped. "I know you can't leave."

But they were at the glass front doors a second later. He moved to the first of them and pressed a palm flat against it, applying pressure until the whole works shattered at once. He did the same to the outer ring, then stood to survey all those UV-intensive mercury vapor lights JJ had told them about.

They came on at sunset, and it seemed the sun had already set.

The lights were humming. Yellow-blue, tinging green — but definitely not on all the way yet.

"Perfect timing," he said.

Then, with the vapor lights still warming up, he dragged his charges through the still-dark plaza, into the darkness, and was gone.

TWENTY
I CAN HEAR

The lights! The damn plaza lights!

JJ felt stupid the second he realized what had happened, and how his maker had played him for a fool. At first, though, he didn't see the ruse. He gave chase, following Arek over the railing to the floor of the theater, falling past the placed ladder and seeing it from his descending perspective as something launched skyward. Falling was slower than running and Arek was encumbered with two human women, so when JJ hit the floor he thought he still had a chance — especially since Arek wouldn't be able to leave. The delusion lasted until he remembered what time it was. The sun had just set, only a minute or two ago. And that meant the lights around the building were just now ...

That's when he realized. Mercury vapor lights, unlike household incandescents, don't just click right on.

JJ had already decided what he'd see by the time he reached the doors. By then it was too late; what he'd suspected turned out to be true. Between the time the last sun rays crossed the horizon and the time the light-activated mercury vapor lights came on, there was a small window of time — probably less than five minutes — wherein the lights needed to warm up. He should have known. Once, when he'd tried to run from Arek, JJ had protected a cottage using similar lights. That time Arek hadn't needed to cross the ultraviolet. He'd simply stood outside and announced that the maker bond compelled JJ to come home — and JJ, still hypnotized, had obeyed. But even then JJ had noticed that low-power window, during which the mercury vapor lights were safe. Apparently Arek had noticed it, too.

"He left?" said Orlo arriving beside JJ. "But ..." He sputtered with indignation. "But that's *cheating!*"

"He never meant to play the game. He just told us he wanted to 'play for it' so he could bide his time until the next sunset. His plan was always to take them and run."

"But how ...?"

JJ explained. He did so quickly, because new handwriting was forming on the wall: They'd have to go after him. When they'd found the necromancer's tome at Elia Sesh's home, at first the whole thing had just seemed annoying: Arek allowed to live forever, and one girl would have to sacrifice to make it happen. But the longer JJ sat with the idea of his maker gaining true immortality — after they found the LARP tournament with Arcadia registered, when it started to seem like the elixir might actually happen — the more he worried. Arek was cruel now; how cruel would he be after another thousand years? How many people would he kill or torture? What's more, immortality struck JJ as a means for Arek, not an end. Step One was to live forever, but then what about Step Two? What would Arek *do* with all that time, all that invulnerability? Arek definitely enjoyed power. It worried JJ what kinds of power he might seek once he had all the time in the world to find it.

Lately, JJ had been possessed with a more close-to-home

set of worries. The fastest way to gain power and favor wasn't to seize it. It was to bargain for power that already existed. That, to JJ, meant that Arek's ultimate goal was probably to impress the Vampire Council. That meant allying with Logan. If Arek became immortal, he might just walk up to their leader in broad sunlight and say to Logan as he hid in the shadows, *Look at me. I have something you want. What will you give me, in order to have it, too?*

And what would happen *then*, once it wasn't just Arek who was immortal? Once other vampires found their Arcadias and made their own elixirs using the incantation? What would the world be like, once Logan and the Vampire Council couldn't die?

JJ's eyes moved to the plaza lights. They were brighter now, starting to flicker. Because JJ wasn't carrying a human who might be killed by excessive G-force, he could zip through full-power lights at top speed and live. It'd hurt, though. Best to go now.

A brown form walked right past JJ and into the light outside. The smell of frying bacon filled the air. It was Rohit, and he was starting to sizzle.

JJ pulled him back. Rohit was adjusting his back, stretching into his knitted bones. He seemed unsurprised that a sledgehammered spine hadn't killed him and seemed not to notice his blistered skin until giant boils formed ... then slowly healed.

"Ultraviolet," JJ explained. "You're a night owl now."

"Oh, snap," said Rohit.

There was no time to explain. Rohit was a vampire now; he'd survive the acceleration just fine. Without pausing to explain (those lights weren't getting any dimmer), JJ grabbed him in a bear hug and ran as fast as he could. A blink later they were outside the apron, near an eerily quiet city street, beneath a pergola. Rohit was throwing up. Rapid acceleration got the newbies every time.

When he recovered, he looked around. The convention center was a memory, lit like a party island viewed from a boat at sea. JJ peeked beyond the pergola, wondering why there weren't more lights. Most streetlights were just fine on vampire skin, but their absence now was almost suspicious.

"Don't you need the others?"

JJ wanted to say no, but some instinct had already caused him to grab Rohit before the ultraviolet window closed. Of course he needed help — but more than that, some small presence inside him was unwilling to be alone. Was it pathetic? Or was it something JJ hadn't been in half a century: a need to be human?

"They'll find us."

"How?"

Rohit's phone buzzed. Strange to be interrupted by something so mundane at a moment like this.

"Ah," he said. "This is Orlo. I'll tell him where we are." He looked around and must have had some idea of their location, because he responded right away. After returning Orlo's text, he moved to pocket the phone. He was shoving it into his jacket when it cracked loudly. Rohit raised his hand, surprised to see a clutch of smashed plastic and metal where his device had so recently been.

"Vampire-strength grip," JJ explained. "Tip of the iceberg."

"But will it get me chicks?"

JJ didn't really hear him and hence didn't answer. He was scanning the area, looking for signs: anything at all that might tell them where Arek had gone. JJ was adjusting on the fly, totally unprepared for the job facing him. He'd assumed they were all playing fair: Win Day Two of the

Vampire Dominion tournament, then go on to Day Three. Their prospects had looked good, with just one other intact team remaining. But now they were back at zero, and Arek could be anywhere by now.

It took a full five more minutes for the others to arrive, but they all came: Brody, Jaden, Orlo, Robert, and Amelie, who looked woozy from blood loss from the twin punctures on her neck. Jason had joined the group, too. It felt like an eternity of time, and once they were all assembled, Arek's whereabouts seemed like they might be farther than ever.

"Think," said Orlo.

"Oh, good one, Orlo," said Brody.

"Excuse me?"

"Just ... great suggestion. He probably hadn't thought of *thinking*."

"You got a problem, Brody?"

"Hey, hey," said Robert.

Brody turned on Robert. "That's it. Make peace. Just stand back there and make sure everyone's getting along."

"What the fuck's the matter with you?" Orlo asked.

"Oh, I don't know," said Brody. "Sucks what happened back there. I mean, if only we'd put guards outside."

That lit Orlo right back up. "Wait, so this is our fault?"

"Weren't you at the door?" He looked at Robert. "Both of you?"

"Easy. We're all doing our best," said Jason Guerey.

Brody spun on Jason. "Really. We are, huh?"

"Hey, we came to rescue you!" Jason shot back. "That other guy just left Rohit behind to ..."

"Hey, hey," said Rohit. "I was doing just fine without—"

"Guys," said Amelie.

"You know, the way I see it," Jason said, "this is *your* problem."

"He took your teammate!" Orlo said, turning on Jason. "She's the reason he's here at all!"

"Bullshit!"

"Guys."

"It's true!" said Orlo. "Tell him, JJ! Tell him about how your buddy wants to live forever, and to do it he needs blood from—"

"Please! He took *your* friends first!"

"Because he made a mistake! Because he was looking for your ..." Orlo seemed to run out of gas. His face was blood-red in the scant illumination of tiny white lights run around the pergola and the park behind. It was too much input; Orlo didn't know where to put all this emotion. It came out in a pointless snap: "Why didn't you use her name! We all knew *your* motherfucking name!"

"Wait. What? Are you mad at me for—?"

"Hippolyta! *Arcadia!* What, you never use her real name, ever? What, do you just vanish into a fantasy world where she's a goddamn Egyptian princess, and—"

"Amazonian," Jaden corrected.

"—and just never come out into the real world, where knowing her goddamn real name would have maybe kept us from sticking our dicks out into the—"

"Oh, this coming from *Shadow Stalker?* Where's your magic hammer, big man? Where's your big, important shit out here in the *real world?*"

"Guys!"

It was Amelie, interrupting for the third time. By the time JJ finally took his attention from the bickering humans and looked her way, she looked pale like paper. She'd gone from standing to leaning, but now faltered and almost fell.

Hands moved to hold her, but she shook her head to

send them back. She held up a hand: *I'll be fine.* But seeing her so drained and weak did, at least, stop the bickering.

"I swear I can hear Nora," she said.

JJ perked his ears, then shook his head. "I don't hear anything."

"I can hear her," Amelie insisted.

"Any of you hear anything?" asked Robert, but it was pointless: JJ's ears were a million times better, and he heard nothing but normal city noise. The humans tried anyway, cocking heads to a gently stirring wind. It was cool out. Enough to make the others' breath — but not JJ's — puff in front of their mouths.

JJ didn't want to say that blood loss was making Amelie delusional, but the question died anyway. They all looked from one to the other, JJ feeling totally outmaneuvered. He had to congratulate Arek. He'd concocted a plan JJ could no longer combat, and they'd swallowed it hook, line, and sinker. As to what to do next, JJ knew only that Arek couldn't be far yet. He had two humans with him; he could only run so fast. But he could take a cab. Or an Uber. He could get on a train. Even walking, they'd be getting farther away by the minute ... and JJ, who had a 360-degree buffet around him, didn't have a clue which direction to head.

"How do we find them?" Rohit asked.

"I don't think we do." And that was a problem. A problem for Nora and Arcadia, but also a problem for the sane part of the vampire world. Logan's beliefs had once been the minority, but now almost every vampire in America would have agreed: Vampires were the elite; vampires were the superior beings. Vampires hadn't always thought that way, but after so long under Logan, elitists comprised most of those turned. If Logan ruled forever and couldn't be usurped, it wouldn't be long before everyone thought like Arek and few thought like JJ. They'd be the new Aryans. There'd be war. A holocaust that'd change day to night. It might take five years. It might take five hundred. But with a regime like Logan's in power forever, it'd happen as sure as sunset.

"Where did he take them, JJ?" Jaden asked. "Think!"

"Consecrated ground," JJ said, remembering. "He needs consecrated ground for the ritual. Now that he's sure, he'll find a Catholic church. Maybe a cemetery."

"Okay," said Jason, pulling up a maps app on his phone. "That helps. We look for churches."

"But even with them, he could be anywhere by now."

"Not *anywhere*," said Orlo. But he trailed off, because he was only hoping that was true.

"Anywhere in the tri-state area," JJ replied.

"I swear," Amelie said again, "that I can *hear her*."

It gave JJ an idea.

Tri-state.

Tri.

I swear that I can hear her.

"I know what to do," JJ told them.

Nora's brain was working overtime.

At first, it'd nearly shut down. All the crazy and all the peril had hit her grey orb's off switch as sure as anything, turning her into the limp sack Arek had dragged from the balcony to the theater floor, through the doors and into the streets. During that time, she'd let her thoughts drift into timeless awareness. Ironically, it was the first time she remembered being in the moment. When Nora looked into the past, it made her sad. When she looked into the future, it gave her heartburn and anxiety. Her parents, friends, teachers, advisors, co-workers, and Starbucks barista kept telling her to relax. To chill out. Even the barista, Nora suspected, had begun slipping her decaf.

Right now, though, her rushing mind (powered back up the minute they'd entered the church) was a blessing. The onslaught of thoughts and desire for order — her Type-A worst — was comfortable like a warm blanket. If she focused on it enough, she could even forget the wrought iron Arek had bent around her wrists like handcuffs. He didn't trust glamouring after his failures at the convention center, so he'd restrained Nora along one wall and tied Hippolyta (whose real name seemed to be Arcadia) at the foot of the altar's crucifix. Arcadia, also unglamoured, kept glancing Nora's way. Her eyes seemed to ask what to do and how they'd get out of here. Surprisingly Arcadia didn't look any more frightened than Nora felt. Maybe they were both in shock. Or maybe they just didn't believe any of this. It was too weird to be real.

Arek moved away after checking both sets of bindings, then headed toward an alcove by the big front doors.

"You don't have red hair," Nora said after he was gone.

"What?"

"He thought his descendent would be a redhead. That's why he took Amelie." Then Nora remembered that Arcadia wasn't part of their guild; she wouldn't know what they were talking about. Did she even understand that Arek was a vampire? It'd taken Nora, after all, so long to admit it. "Wait. Do you ..."

"Jason and I have been following you all day. Yes. We know."

"And you ... *believe?*"

"I don't think I'd LARP if I hadn't halfway believed from the beginning."

Nora looked at Arcadia, envying how simple she made belief sound. As a child, Nora hadn't believed in Santa, or the Tooth Fairy, or even that the pipes under the sink went into a septic tank until Dad had taken her into the basement and shown her. All Nora's life, wonder had taken a backseat to evidence: *If you can't prove it, it doesn't exist.* Life itself, for Nora, was guilty until proven innocent. The idea that all Hippolyta — *Arcadia,* now that they were prison buddies — had to do in order to believe was to *see* wasn't only foreign to Nora. It was downright exciting. Logic was a harsh mistress, and sometimes she wondered what it'd be like to simply *let go*.

"It'd dyed," Arcadia said.

"What?"

"My hair. I dye it. I'm naturally redder than your friend."

"Why would you do that?" Nora had never been happy with much about her appearance. People told her she was pretty "in her own special way," but to Nora "special" sounded like an adjective used for those who were strange or broken, just to make them feel better. Her face was ordinary. Her haircut was boring and utilitarian. Once, when Robert had asked her out, she'd assumed he was joking. The idea that someone could have such a unique and beautiful asset as long red hair and just bury it? Well, that was beyond odd to Plain Old Nora.

"Maybe we can discuss beauty tips when we're out of here?" Arcadia said.

"Of course. I'm sorry."

Nora clammed up when she saw activity from the alcove, but Arek was just moving to another part of the church.

"Do you know where we are?" Nora asked.

Arcadia shook her head. "I'm not from around here. I live in Naperville. It's—"

"I know," Nora interrupted. "That's where Jason lives."

"Oh. Right. I forgot you were friends."

"'Friends' might be overstating it," Nora said. And that, ironically, was an understatement. Outwardly, Nora's guild had always been friendly with Jason's when they met in the outside world. It made sense because outside, there were no guilds — just people with normal lives and normal jobs and normal worries about money and relationships. Yet when the guild was together without others around, you'd think Jason and his friends were the Devil. It all seemed so stupid now — now that there was *real* peril in the world. On the biggest level, they should have been allies because they were all human. Below that, even, they should have been allies because they were all off of the mainstream: America, as a whole, thought LARPers were weird. Yet had they focused on what was the same? Never. The human brain was most adept at pointing out what was different.

Arcadia looked up. Nora, with her organized mind, had already done several comprehensive sweeps of their surroundings. She didn't need to follow Arcadia's gaze to remember the way you could see sky through the ceiling.

"This place looks abandoned," Arcadia said.

Travel had been a literal blur. Nora only remembered snippets of her trip with Arek, and in general she didn't know if they'd come a mile or a hundred miles. "I know we came through a bunch of construction. I saw construction by the expressway ..."

Arcadia shrugged. "Of course, that's assuming we're even still in Detroit. But even if we are, there seems to be construction everywhere."

"Assuming we're still in Detroit," Nora repeated. She had to believe they were; otherwise she'd go crazy. If they were a state away, then they were dead. No question about it if Arek had truly lost the others.

They were silent. Nora's brain was still looking for weaknesses. None were obvious. The stained-glass windows were boarded and their arrival had been a whirlwind. She could see no landmarks that might indicate their location. The vampire, before binding them, had taken their cell phones and watches — even a little FitBit Nora kept in her pocket to count her steps. Anything that might give up their location, he'd taken — and smashed, judging by the commotion they'd heard the last time he'd left the sanctuary.

"It's Camille?" Arcadia asked. Her voice was a little softer now. They'd left the wiseass place, where jokes and wry observations might be allowed. Having determined they had no idea where they were or how they'd ever get out, what remained was far more dour. This was an actual life or death situation. Which one of the women was in more danger — the sacrifice, or the witness — was still up for grabs.

"Nora," Nora said. "My *character's* name is Camille."

"I'm happy to meet you, Nora."

"I'm happy to meet you too, Arcadia. Officially, I mean." They'd been acquainted as characters for more than 24 hours now. This was a whole new angle on a dicey situation.

In a still-smaller voice, Arcadia said, "What's he going to do with us, do you think?"

Oh. Poor thing. She didn't know. She hadn't blinked at the "ancestor" comment earlier, but she must have figured it was tangential — extra information, not info that really mattered. So, as kindly as she could, Nora explained what JJ had told them.

"Oh," Arcadia said when the story was finished. She was sitting beneath the big cross on the altar, legs in a V in front of her. Her hands, like Nora's hands, were bound behind her back.

"But you don't know how he's supposed to do it?" Arcadia asked a few seconds later.

"I just know he needs your blood. I know there's some sort of incantation. Tell the truth, I don't even think *he* knows for sure. I'll bet that's why he took so long with Amelie — just trying to figure it out."

"Maybe he *won't* figure it out," Arcadia said.

Nora nodded, but that wasn't actually an encouraging thought. If things went smoothly, Arek would be in a good mood. If they didn't, he would probably be angry. Either way, Nora didn't think he'd just let them go. But it did, now that she considered it, kind of give her an idea. She looked around.

"What are you looking for?"

"JJ said there was a book."

"So what?"

"He said it was in symbols."

"Hieroglyphics?"

Nora shook her head. "If my compulsive studying is worth anything, I'll bet it's written in ancient runes."

"I don't even know what that is," Arcadia said.

"Of course you don't. Nobody out-geeks me." She said it lightly, but all that studying and learning and living in fantasy had cost her what normal people called a social life. Still, maybe her geekdom was about to pay off.

She was about to speak, but stopped when Arek re-entered the room. He looked from one woman to the other, playing more than genuinely surveying. His face said he knew something they didn't want him to know, and now he intended to have some fun.

"Why were you talking about my book?" he asked.

Nora felt caught. Of course he had super-hearing. She tried to recall all that she and Arcadia had discussed and decided she'd given nothing away. Thank God she hadn't spoken her new idea out loud.

"I just ... I think I've heard of it, is all," Nora lied. Then she repeated random things JJ had said, hoping Arek wouldn't ask for specifics: "Written by a human necromancer. Big, heavy thing, right? Written in runes?"

Arek nodded, but he no longer looked playful. His expression now was genuinely curious.

"I've studied it," Nora said. "I was interested. But if all you're going to do is kill us ..."

Arek interrupted. "What do you know?"

At his invitation, Nora uncorked entirely. She spared no embarrassment, holding back none of her nerd knowledge. The words she said probably meant something, but the way she threaded them together was pure hand-waving bullshit: the kind of flim-flam a magician does to draw the audience's eye to something that means nothing. And, just like a magician, all that verbal garbage had a reason: It was a distraction. It was camouflage. It was attention drawn to the left hand so the audience won't notice what the right hand is doing.

Her diarrhea of buzzwords must have impressed Arek, because he disappeared and came back soon after with a very old book with gold bindings. He flopped it open, holding it for Nora because Nora couldn't hold it herself.

"You're saying you can read this?"

Actually, she could. Sort of. You didn't get to be a renowned Dungeon Master without learning a few runes. So Nora nodded at some of the more obvious characters and read them aloud. Arek, watching, seemed impressed. He closed the book, raising his eyebrows. "Very good," he said.

This next bit would be delicate. Nora needed Arek to think it was his idea instead of hers, but he'd thought showing her the book was his idea ... so: *So far, so good.*

"Who's going to read the incantation for you?" she asked.

"What?"

"Wasn't that an incantation?" She nodded at the book in his hands. She'd affected nonchalance, even though the subject was anything but. "It said something about immortality, and there was an incantation."

"*Riiight* ..." Arek said.

"So, what ... I guess you have friends coming? So someone can read the incantation?"

Arek looked confused. Nora said, "Wait. You weren't planning to read it yourself, were you?"

"Well ..."

"You can't necromance *for* yourself *by* yourself!" she said, trying a small laugh. It sounded a little superior, but if she wanted to seem like she had superior knowledge, a little cockiness was required. "If that's how it worked, demons would just summon themselves!"

Arek seemed annoyed by her tone, but still respectful of it. He looked more like he didn't *want* to believe her than actually disbelieving.

"Bullshit."

"Hey, if you don't believe me, just read the page. It's right there in ink."

Arek stepped back as if wary of a trap. Kicking at Arek would be the height of folly and they both knew it, but he still didn't look like he meant to take chances. Out of kicking range, he opened the book and said, "Where?"

"At the bottom."

"I don't see anything like that."

"Jesus. Come on. I can see it from here."

He came closer, forgetting his suspicion. "Show me."

Nora did the best she could to point with her chin and nose, since her hands were bound.

"Here?" His finger on the page.

"Below that."

"Here?"

"The line starting with the squiggly thing. See?"

She was pretty sure the line of symbols at the bottom was just decorative. "I can't read this," he said.

"Really?"

"You're saying you can?"

"Come on. *Runes, Klingon* ... How many languages do *you* speak?"

He was surprised enough to actually answer: "One."

"Which one?"

"English."

"Oh. So you really meant *one.*"

"Are you insulting me?"

Nora decided it was time for a bit more acting. She had to be scared, which would come naturally, but she also had to limit that fear and feign confidence, which would be harder.

"Look. It's Arek?"

Arek nodded.

"I've never been more scared in my life, Arek. But I'm a practical person. I'm thinking maybe if I help you, you'll ..."

"... help *you?*"

Nora made her face bashful. Deferent. "Maybe you'll let me live."

"I see. That's what you think?" He moved closer. From the corner of her eye, Nora could see Arcadia, her face wondering just what the hell Nora was up to.

Nora swallowed and nodded. "You can glamour me. Make me forget so I don't tell anyone what happened here."

"I'm not the best at that. At glamouring."

"I'd never tell! Why would I tell? Nobody would believe me!"

Arek seemed to be considering. He looked from the

book to Nora, Nora to the book. Then he said, "You can read runes."

She nodded.

"You can read this incantation?"

She nodded again. She could just sound it out, which was probably what Arek had been intending.

"And what does *this* say?" He pointed where she'd indicated: the crap she'd said were words, but that was probably just decoration.

"'And so shall the seeker have spoken the words from a distance, from one anointed.'"

"'From a distance,'" Arek repeated.

"Yes."

He looked down, doubting. "Read it again."

Shit. She hadn't counted on having to recall her bullshit word for word. He was smarter than she thought.

"'And so the seeker shall be told from a distance, from someone anointed.'"

"That's not what you said the first time."

Double shit. Time to go on the offensive. Arrogance was better than being dead.

"What, you think it's a literal translation?" Nora said, her voice haughty. "If you're such a linguist, you fucking read it!"

Arek considered her for another moment, neither angry nor accepting. He was somewhere in between.

"All right," he said. "If you'll read the incantation, I'll let you go."

"You promise?"

"Not at all," he said. "But what choice do you have?"

Ugh. This could be going better. But at least the core of her idea was still intact. She could buy time, but that was all.

"I need to be anointed."

"How?"

"Holy water, I assume."

"I'm not a big fan of holy water," Arek said.

"Then untie me, and I'll anoint myself."

Arek reached into Nora's pocket. Neurotic as she was, there was always a small tube of toothpicks inside. Arek dumped them on the floor, then held up the case. It'd make a perfect little cup, so long as he held it by the attached cap to avoid touching the water with his fingers.

"Just a second," he said.

"What are you doing?" Arcadia hissed when Arek seemed out of earshot.

But because he probably *wasn't* out of earshot, Nora lied: "I'm going to give him what he wants."

Tri-state.

Tri.

Triangle.

Triangulation.

From what JJ explained to Amelie, feeding connected a vampire to his prey for a brief window of time, thanks to an unavoidable intermingling of blood. Sometimes a human would feel vampire abilities but not actually have them. Sometimes she'd feel the presence of another mind inside her own, almost like being possessed. And sometimes, like in Amelie's case, a transient psychic bond caused a person to hear what the vampire heard and sense what the vampire sensed, even if they were miles apart. The bond passed in hours, but for now JJ assured Amelie that what she believed was actually true: She *was* hearing Nora, through Arek's ears.

By itself, the bond was useless. JJ couldn't forcibly connect to his maker's mind, so Amelie's connection — thousands of times weaker — couldn't even come close. But still Amelie had a *sense* of Arek, and JJ had a sense of Arek, and Rohit, who was also Arek's progeny, had a sense of Arek. Any one bond told them nothing ... but all three, used together, had potential.

Under the protection of darkness, JJ took Orlo's phone and ran halfway across the city. Rohit, who was just now learning his vampire abilities, borrowed Robert's phone and went as far as he could in a different direction. Amelie, still human, remained where she was with her own phone. Five minutes later they were on a three-way call, following JJ's instructions.

"Nothing," said Amelie.

"Nothing," said Rohit.

She heard the sounds of shuffled paper: a big Detroit map JJ had snatched from a gas station. He read off new intersections, new directions. After a few minutes JJ and Rohit were in new locations, still spread out in a massive, roughly equilateral triangle across the city.

Amelie focused inside, waiting for the faint echo of Nora's voice to grow louder.

"Nothing," she said again. "It's the same as before."

"Same for me," said Rohit.

JJ gave them new coordinates, again and again. The two vampires — JJ and Rohit — were sweeping around Amelie in a giant circle, keeping her in the center as the triangle's third point.

"Okay," said Rohit after their fifth shuffle. "I'm here."

"Go ahead, Amelie," said JJ.

Amelie closed her eyes, shutting out the waiting faces of Orlo, Jaden, Brody, Robert, and Jason. She heard Nora's voice instantly, but this time it was different.

"She sounds louder," Amelie said into the phone.

"Louder how?" JJ sounded encouraged but reserved, holding his judgment.

"Like an echo."

"Keep listening. Tell me if it grows."

Amelie listened again to her thoughts. It was a strange thing, hearing someone else where your own ideas should be. But yes. Nora was still there — and she was growing louder.

"She's still getting louder," Amelie said. "But it's still all mumbly. I can't hear what she's saying."

"Rohit?" said JJ.

"Yes! I can hear her now, too!" His voice dropped a little. "But it's the same deal as Amelie. I can tell it's her, but I can't hear the words."

"That's normal. All three of us are actually hearing Arek, not Nora. We're hearing her *through* Arek. He has his own defenses." There was a rustling pause, and Amelie imagined JJ shaking the issue away. "It's not important. Give me a second. Nobody talk."

JJ took maybe three minutes, but it felt like forever. In the quiet, Amelie found herself remembering all the peril around them. She'd shut it out while she'd had jobs to do: *Escape, don't pass out, listen for Nora's voice to grow as the triangulation does its job.* But now, in stillness, the fact of Nora's (and Arcadia's) imprisonment was coming back to her. They could die. All of them, if they kept going with this, could die. Her friend Rohit, who she'd known for years, was now a vampire. *A vampire!* It was more than impossible to believe, so she set it aside for later.

"I have him," JJ said. "I know where he is!"

Amelie was picturing the map. She didn't know Detroit. Bridge to Windsor, I-75 running up from Toledo like Michigan's carotid artery ... that was about it. What's more, she'd lost track of where Rohit and JJ were now, so she couldn't picture the triangle they'd made. What was inside it? Upon which sacred ground was Arek holding her friends?

"So ...?" Amelie said into the phone.

"Hamtramck," said JJ, arriving in-the-flesh behind her. "Let's go."

TWENTY-THREE
BLUSTER AND FLAME

Nora could only bluster so long. As her bullshit began to fatigue, she started to wonder if this had been a good idea. When she'd come up with the idea, it'd felt genius. Now it struck her like a kid deliberately missing the school bus. What, did she think her mom wouldn't just drive her to school, and she'd have to go anyway? Had she really thought that missing the bus would solve the problem, rather than simply delaying the inevitable?

In the same way, did she really think that bullshitting through Arek's ritual would change the future? He was already frustrated, now growing madder and madder. He wasn't going to give up, and any chance at good will she'd felt when she'd told him she'd help was already gone. Maybe, if Nora had kept her mouth shut and just let Arek do what he'd wanted to do, this would be over already. Arek might have glamoured and released them both; he might have glamoured and released Arcadia; he might have killed them both or done some combination of the above. But at least it'd be over. It wouldn't still be dragging on ... with no respite in sight.

Every time the ritual failed, Arek's mood got worse. JJ had told them he had a temper, but only now was Nora starting to see its raw edge. If things went on this way much longer (and really, there was no way they couldn't), Arek wouldn't glamour them and let them go. He also wouldn't just kill them. Right now, given his mood, he'd probably suck them dry like Capri Sun pouches, then cut them up while they were still alive. He'd make sure they found a horrible way to die.

"This isn't working," Arek said.

"You need to drink *while* I'm reading," Nora said.

She was running out of variations to suggest, but her frustration was nothing compared to Arcadia's obvious discomfort. Every time Arek went back to drink more, he re-punctured her neck wounds. They looked raw and sore, and Arcadia's eyes were leaking tears of pain.

"I've *been* drinking while you're reading!" Arek complained.

"Yeah, but it says you have to do it with a calm mind."

Nora glanced back at the open book on its stand, inspired by her own words. That last lie could be useful. Arek had a hot temper and would find it hard to calm down now that he was riled up. But it sounded good; "calm mind" was just Buddhist enough to be believable. It would take a while for him to get calm, if he even could. More time to stall, more time to think of a way out.

"How do I get a calm mind?"

"I don't know. Breathe deeply."

As Arek did his Yogi impression and closed his eyes, Nora again looked at Arcadia. Both women were still bound, Arcadia's entire right side now soaked in her own blood. The wound seemed to seal between bites, but she was still flagging, owing to Arek's sloppy way of drinking.

She didn't see Nora's look of apology this time, nor a look Nora hoped looked like disobedient determination. Probably just as well, since Nora had no idea what exactly she was disobeying *for*. They were already dead. The best Nora could hope was to keep it possible that Arek could die, too.

"Okay," said Arek, breathing artificially slow. "Make it work this time."

"That's not up to me," Nora said.

"Try," he told her, "because if you can't help, you're of no use to me."

Nora swallowed. It wasn't an act this time.

"Read more slowly," he said.

Nora nodded.

Arek lowered himself over Arcadia. She tried to roll away, but she'd lost a lot of strength. When he sunk in, Nora heard a nauseating sound like biting into the soft flesh of a peeled orange. Arcadia moaned in pain.

Nora watched Arek's throat, watching for him to begin drinking. When she saw his Adam's apple bob and a fresh glut pour into Arcadia's blouse, Nora read the incantation incorrectly again. She kept omitting the same word, hoping a small change would be enough to botch the ritual. The only problem was, she'd read the wrong line ten or more times by now. By now, Arek knew the short incantation by heart — and that meant if he looked at the book, it'd be obvious that Nora was failing on purpose. She'd go from useless to a saboteur, and he'd kill her on the spot.

Predictably, nothing happened. Arek pulled back and stood straight as if he might suddenly feel invigorated (the "elixir" sounded more like a concept than something you held in your hand), but he must not have. He looked again at Nora.

"I'm sorry," she said.

Arek had looked calm before. Now he looked furious and out of patience. With his fangs out and his lips bloodied, he practically growled, "You're doing this on purpose."

"I'm not doing anything!"

"You're playing with me."

"I'm just reading what's here! If you want to blame someone, blame—!"

Arek was in front of her as quickly as snapping fingers. His hand was cocked back, and he let it fly with superhuman speed. Nora, tethered, had no way to block. She rattled against her restraints, cheek hot and momentarily numb.

"I'll do it myself," he said.

"The runes say someone else has to do it."

"I'll take my chances."

He shoved Nora roughly aside. She was still cuffed, but that didn't last long; skin ripped as his push yanked both wrists through her iron restraints. She hit the floor, free but buried in agony. The backs of both hands gushed from thick severed veins. She looked like a kid with convertible winter gloves: all she'd have to do, to cover her exposed fingers, would be to wrap the flaps of hanging skin over them.

Nora screamed. Arek ignored her.

She wanted to run, but the pain was so intense, even fight-or-flight wouldn't push her upright. She felt her glands as empty sacks: all that adrenaline already spent on the world's most hideous weekend. When she tried to rise, she stumbled. The world upended and then canted sideways, the indoor horizon rising drunkenly to stand.

She hit the stone floor head-first, sidelong at the temple. *You just got a concussion,* a part of her mind told her, *and you're bleeding from the head.* But she didn't have time for that, seeing as she was about to die.

Arek went to the book, pulling it from its stand. His eyes scanned the page. Then he looked hard at Nora.

Well, shit.

"You've been reading this wrong."

Nora tried to sit up. Her world was spinning. She only managed a partial word: *"Nuh."*

"You've been reading it wrong *on purpose.*"

"I—"

Arek snapped closer. *Much* closer. He had her by the throat. Now Nora couldn't even say partial words. All that came out was a gagging sound.

"What does it say, at the bottom?"

Arek's fingers, already on her neck, seemed to pop inward as if breaking through an obstruction. Had he just snapped her neck muscles? Would she be able to hold her head up?

He held the old book against her face like a naughty dog rubbed in his own business. His voice was like broken glass.

"What does it say?"

Nora gurgled. It was getting harder to breathe.

Arek released his grip, holding her neck more lightly now. "At the bottom. The line about someone else reading it. Tell me what it really says."

She couldn't remember. Her lie was too arbitrary, impossible to recall word for word. She searched her memory, but Arek noted the place Nora was searching for answers: the upper-right corner of her vision, not the book in front of her. She wasn't trying to *read.* She was trying to *recall.*

Arek roared, slammed her head against the stone, and threw the book across the room. The slam was not light; Nora felt more of her skull break.

"I should pull you apart," he said. "Piece by piece."

"Don't, though," said a new voice.

Nora rolled her eyes to see JJ standing at the threshold. The picture lasted only a second, because a blip later JJ was gone, striking Arek like a weighty bullet. Both vampires flew across the sanctuary to break a star-shaped pattern in the stones of the outer wall.

Arek parried, using momentum to spin JJ by the arms. Nora must have lost consciousness for a blip then because what came next was impossible: The second JJ's feet again touched the ground, he took his maker by the underside of the chin and pressed fingers through the floor of his mouth to hold Arek's jawbone like a handle. With a heave, JJ then whipped Arek up and over his head using that handle, slamming Arek flat on his other side.

The others came, but Nora barely saw them. She was moving in and out of the world, sure she was bleeding, sure she was spiraling into darkness. How badly had she been wounded? She couldn't move her hands. A thick, coppery-smelling something licked across her cheek, filling her senses. It was her own blood, spreading thick like syrup, dark crimson like burnt brick.

Arek pedaled back like a crab, now eyeing all the humans who'd come with JJ. Swimming through fog, Nora saw all her friends: Orlo, who she loved by never dared declare herself to, Amelie, who made her jealous but had always fought for her, Jaden who was learned and Robert who was pure of heart, Brody who was loyal, and Rohit, their jester — their strong man now, who'd never see the sun.

As she looked at them, she distinctly thought: *Why do we play in a fantasy world? The real world is quest enough.*

Arek's eyes went to the human group at the door, but JJ stood to guard them. So instead, Arek zipped to Arcadia.

He crouched behind her, then carefully unbound her with his eyes on JJ, daring the other to make a move. They both stood, and Arek began to backpedal with his human shield.

"I'm taking her," he said.

JJ shook his head. "Take her blood if you must. But leave *her*, Arek."

Arek snarled. "Immortality awaits me."

"We are immortal enough. Only you would want more."

"*We aren't immortal!*" Arek snapped. "We are fallible! We are hunted by these ... *things! They* hunt *us!*"

"It is a two-way street," JJ said. "It's only under Logan that vampires refuse to consider peace."

Arek's vampire teeth grated. He dragged Arcadia's ragdoll body in arcs to keep her in front of him. "*Peace,*" he growled.

"Let her go, Arek."

"Why?"

"Because if you take her, I will never stop following you. Never stop hunting you. You can't hide from me forever. I will always be around the corner, do you understand? You will never lay down at sunrise and be certain you'll wake."

Arek re-gripped Arcadia, now eyeing a window that was only partially boarded. He was going to leap for it. They were about to lose them both.

"*Don't,* Arek. This is your chance to think. To do what's right for a change."

But Arek was hearing none of it. He'd become the victim here; it wasn't his fault. "Why would you do this?" he whined to JJ. "Why would you turn your back on your kind?"

"Because my kind turned its back on me."

Arek grew more furious. "I made you perfect. I made

you strong. We had an agreement, JJ! What's mine is yours. What's yours is mine. We're connected, you and me! We have a bond! Does it mean nothing to you?"

JJ slowly put his hand in his mouth. His entire fist wouldn't fit, but he could tent the fingers like the end of a rocket — a flesh-and-blood RPG pointed at his brain from the inside.

Arek's face faltered. "What ... What the hell are you doing?"

JJ removed the hand long enough to speak. "I've always wondered. How *much* can you feel my pain?"

Arek saw what JJ intended all at once. He moved to spring, raising one hand toward his progeny. His fingers were splayed, every motion in slow-motion. Nora looked to JJ then, missing all of this, unsure why what JJ just said mattered. But then, when JJ did what he intended, it all came clear.

The maker bond. JJ had told Nora all about it as they'd talked alone throughout the day. The blood connection between vampires didn't compel the new one to obey, but it did connect one to the other. The bond was unavoidable empathy: forced pain with a steel fist.

In one powerful motion, JJ drove his tented hand upward like the blast of a shotgun. His vampire muscles forced the hand up through bone and into brain, out the back of his head in an exit wound of spraying tissue. Nora found the strength to whimper, watching her new friend's head explode and his body collapse.

But JJ hadn't done it for suicide. He'd done it because the bond turned his pain into Arek's pain.

Arek screeched like nothing Nora had heard before. His muscles went lax, allowing Arcadia, frail as she was, to drop from his grip. She did so with a flop and a crawl, but by then

Arek was stumbling back, unsure where to grab because everything hurt. It wasn't his own head that had exploded or his own brain that was no more ... but still the pain, still the torment. He gripped head and stomach, gripped mouth with fingers and thumb. He collapsed, rolling in panic and pain.

Brody rushed in. Orlo rushed in. They all rushed in, carrying small objects they must have run back to the tournament to procure. Seeing it, a confused thought ran through Nora's flagging mind: *It must have taken all their points to get those, and now we'll never win.*

Every human at the door was holding an ultraviolet palm beacon like the one Arcadia, as Hippolyta, had used the first time they'd met. Unlike fake silver stakes and other LARP doodads, the ultraviolet lights were real: small sunlamps probably meant to treat Seasonal Affective Disorder. They were cheap things, buyable at a Dollar Store. What reason was there for the tournament to use fakes, when real ones were inexpensive and safe? After all, it's not like vampires existed.

Under the blast of five UV lights, Arek cowered. After that he screamed, skin sizzling like a steak on a griddle. Nora, still immobile, saw his face bubble with huge black boils. When he collapsed, it was Orlo who rushed closer, ripping Arek's shirt open. His newly exposed skin bubbled too, then, accelerating the process.

All at once Arek lit with white-hot flame, burning like the first strike of a road flare. The humans around him stepped back. Sixty seconds later his shirt collapsed into an empty torso, his pants flattening as the rest of his body died. Flakes of black ash filled the air like up-drifting snow.

After that, it was only his clothing that burned.

TWENTY-FOUR
TURN

It could have been ten seconds later. Maybe a minute. Maybe an hour, maybe ten. Nora had fallen asleep and she didn't know where. Nor did she understand why, when she opened her eyes, she saw a man she seemed to remember only from a dream.

"You are dying," the man said.

Nora found she could answer. Was she on the floor? No, no, bigger question: Was she *in a church?* She remembered something very long ago about a church, and danger, and things she'd seen that could not be. But those strange memories felt very, very far away.

"It's not so bad," Nora told him.

"There is no way to stop your dying," the man told her. "The question is, do you want to live?"

She was resting on her cheek. Across from her, also on the floor, so was he. He was absolutely and completely covered in blood. *So* much blood. Although a lot of it, Nora now noticed, was topped with ash. His hand was both red and black. What had he done — slaughtered a pig, then reached into a fire?

She was remembering, though. Remembering some, but not enough.

"You said there's no way to stop me dying."

"That's right."

"So how can I live?"

"The way I live."

"But ..." She had it. "But *you* died, too. I saw it." She seemed to remember him doing something impossible, his head exploding.

Now she could see the others around her, standing in a circle as if mourning already. She, too, was covered in blood, most of its volume in a pool beneath her. It was warm and smelled like coins. She found she could move her hand and did, discovering a huge wound on her skull — one that felt more like a window, with something soft beneath.

"Wood through the heart," said the vampire. "Silver. Sunlight. That's the way we die."

"But your head ..."

"Brains regrow."

"Were you sure? That you'd live?"

"No," said JJ. "But I decided to trust." He gave a wan smile. "It's never been easy for me to trust."

He sat upright. Nora realized she must only have blacked out for a few seconds, because Arek's clothing was still aflame in the corner. JJ, however, was almost entirely healed. The blood on him was mostly ash. What remained, of hot red blood, was her own.

"I can save you," he said. "I can save you by damning you."

"Damned like you are damned?"

JJ gave a small nod.

"But my body ..."

"Recent wounds heal. It's the old wounds that remain."

She considered. She had enough mind left, even now, to do so. *Become a vampire or die for good.* It was a choice no person in a rational world should have to make.

She looked up at JJ, moving only her eyes. He was smiling just a little: a sad, sober smile that seemed to know the truth of the big, cruel world.

The answer came to her. It was surprising, if not surprising at all.

"I've been half a vampire for years as Camille," she said. "How different can it be to make it real?"

She turned her head as much as she was able, exposing her neck. She didn't know how this worked, but she assumed that to turn her, he'd have to drink.

"Are you sure?" JJ asked.

"No," she said. "But I'm deciding to trust."

TWENTY-FIVE
AWAKE

Nora rose. She felt like a newborn deer at first, uncertain on her legs. By the time she was fully standing, though, all that changed. She was the same old Nora, but new confidence radiated from every inch of her. She was somehow more upright. More poised. More glowing. She looked at Orlo, knowing that of course he knew she loved him ... but *that* had changed, too.

She put fingers to her skull, where previously it'd cracked. "Recent wounds," she said with wonder, feeling only intact skin and bone.

Everyone looked a little shell-shocked. It was hard to fathom how much their lives had upended in the past 36 hours. How would Nora go home now? How would Rohit? But the questions were too big. There would be time for them later.

"What now?" JJ asked.

Surprised looks went around the group. It seemed they'd all assumed he'd know, being the oldest. But this was their world now. The human world. It wasn't blood that made them what they were. It was choice, and community, and belief. And trust.

"We can't go back to the hotel," Orlo said when all those eyes settled on him.

"That's okay," said Jaden. "For the first time in my life, I think I've had enough vampires." Then he looked at JJ, Nora, and Rohit and said, "No offense."

"None taken," said Nora. But she had the distinct, outside-herself impression that she was a little high, probably hopped-up on a new vampire's version of adrenaline. It hadn't registered (not really, because how could it?) that she was something different now. She couldn't live her old life anymore — not really. She thought of all JJ had told her, about how he'd lost his family simply because he was something they were not. Would it be that way for her? Had she answered his life-saving question too rashly?

There was so much she hadn't considered, like the fact that she'd never change from this point on. Never gain weight, never grow older. She now *couldn't* change — at least physically. The way she was today, she'd be that way forever: waif-skinny, flat-chested, maybe-pretty but unremarkable in her own mirror. She ran track so maybe she'd be fast, but what else did she have going? She wasn't strong, or cover-model handsome, or skilled in any particular way. She hadn't trained. She hadn't optimized first, like styling hair before spraying it immobile with VO5. It suddenly felt like she'd woken this morning and tossed on any old clothes, unaware she'd be wearing them forever.

A bolt of panic struck her. She turned to JJ. "We weren't licensed. We weren't approved by your Council." She looked at Rohit and added, "Neither of us."

"I know. But what could I do? If I hadn't turned you, you'd have died."

"But I'm ..." She looked down. She was so completely average. So completely unperfect. "... you know," she finished.

"It's okay," JJ said. "We stopped this." He pointed at Arek's spellbook, which someone had kicked toward Arek's flaming clothes; now it was burning, too. "Only Arek and I know that book exists. Exis*ted*," he corrected. "With it gone, the Council will stay as mortal as our kind can be. Eventually someone will challenge Logan. When they do, things will change."

"How does that help us right now?"

JJ nodded grimly. "It doesn't. We will need a plan. A way to hide you that doesn't seem strange, until the world is different."

"What makes you so sure things will change?" Orlo asked.

"Because they already are," JJ replied. "When it started to seem like Arek would achieve his goal and become immortal, I reached out for help. It was not easy. There are only so many vampires known to think as I do." He looked around; two in his number were now his kind. "As *we* do," he said. "I found one: exactly *one* vampire outspoken enough to challenge the Council, but too old and too powerful — literally and politically — for them to silence. Where there is one, there will be more. Eventually, with enough help, others will speak out as he does."

"Who is the one?"

"His name is Maurice Toussant. He's two thousand years old — easily the most powerful vampire I've ever met."

"You've *met* him?" Nora asked. She didn't want to hope. The picture JJ painted of vampirekind was grim, but the idea of a two-thousand-year-old vampire on their side was too exciting to deny.

"Oh yes," he said. "Just once, but that was enough to know where he stands. What the future holds. And who it is that stands beside him."

Nora looked at Rohit, as if he somehow knew. He shrugged. "Who 'stands beside Maurice'?" she asked JJ.

"His progeny, Reginald."

"What about Reginald?" she asked. "Why does *he* matter?"

"Reginald is the Council's worst nightmare: an unlicensed vampire with unusual potential ... and proof, to the right people, that Logan's way of seeing our world is dead wrong."

Nora and Rohit exchanged a glance. Nora's curiosity was off the charts.

"To be blunt, Reginald is a fat vampire," JJ said, "and you wouldn't *believe* what he can do."

One year later

ARCADIA JANE O'CONNOR stepped in front of the group of wary young adults. She didn't have a microphone. She didn't need one. She knew this routine by heart — and from birth, everyone had told her she was too loud already.

"Hello," she said. "My name is Arcadia and I'll be your Game Master for the afternoon. I know Orlo already gave you all the rules, but I just wanted to hop in real quick before we set y'all loose. How many of you have LARPed before?"

A few hands went up. Too few.

"Right," Arcadia told them. "Well. Let me tell you something. It's a secret."

In the past, she'd asked groups at this point if they'd like to hear her secret. Crowds were always shy, though, so she'd omitted the question and altered her schtick to push right on.

"I know a lot of you have LARPed. A lot more than just

raised your hands. So I know you know the rules, and the rules of our game are pretty much the same — just with the few differences Orlo mentioned. I know that in the game, you know what to do. I know you'll be confident once you're inside. But I also know some of you — maybe a lot of you — are still a little scared. If I'm wrong, tell me. Go ahead. I seriously want to know."

Arcadia smiled to encourage them, but to date nobody had ever raised a hand. Today's lack of hands, therefore, was no surprise. The Blood Mayhem LARP had a very unusual advertising plan, and hence knew exactly who its customers were. Whereas bigger games advertised widely, the game Arcadia had made with her friends was far more targeted, the crowds far more timid.

Only the most introverted people saw their ads: the most socially awkward, yet skilled. A lot of LARPers in other groups were "normal" by society's definition: They looked and acted mainstream. They had mainstream jobs. They dated, married, had mainstream kids and participated in otherwise mainstream-acceptable hobbies. But it wasn't that way for Blood Mayhem. Jaden was excellent at social media, able to craft ads that reached only the most disenfranchised: the geeks of all geeks, in other words. So yes, the groups Arcadia spoke to were always shy and introverted — beaten that way by bullies, peers, and bosses. They didn't tend to speak up or raise hands ... but that was the point, in Arcadia's mind. These people had skills but had been rolled over. They were, to put it elegantly but imprecisely, diamonds in the rough. And that's exactly what they were after, when all was said and done: *uncut diamonds*. They didn't always look pretty, but inside they were the fortunes that others missed.

"It's okay if you're nervous," Arcadia said. "Nervous for

the game, nervous about winning, nervous about interacting with us or the other people around you — doesn't matter. I know you understand what I'm about to say, because it's probably the reason you LARP in the first place. I know it's why I did — why I still do, when I'm able."

Now the crowd was interested. They wanted to know what she was teasing, but also how this pretty woman with the strong backbone and thriving business had ever been — and apparently still was — one of them.

"You're here to be someone else," she said. "So *be that.* Be it to the limit you can be. The more you are true to your character, the truer you are to *you.* My in-game name is Hippolyta. Orlo's? Shadow Stalker. We all met while playing a game, and to this day we all have 'real selves' we often hide. But here's the trick: Hide what you were, not who you are today. We all get to choose who we are. Is anyone bold enough to tell me who they are?"

A brave hand rose — a man with curly black hair in the front row.

"I'm Dave," he said when Arcadia pointed.

"And who are you? What are your special abilities?"

"I'm an engineer. Even without a calculator, I can calculate—"

She held up a hand. "But Dave. Who *are* you?"

"My character is Blowback James. He's a vampire hunter."

"He is?" Arcadia teased. *"Or you are?"*

Dave didn't answer. Still too shy. That was okay. He had facility with numbers; that was good to know. Others, based on their applications, displayed other skills that might come in handy. Some knew lore. Some knew weapons. Some could build. Many were good with computers — something the Vampire Nation was too antiquated to really figure out. Some were bold deep down. Many were brave. Almost all were loyal. Those attributes wouldn't come out in the everyday world, but that was okay. A few would sift through and join them, and thanks to this little rehearsal, there'd be no guesswork. The game was monitored intensely when the LARP was on. Nothing went unseen, either by real eyes or cameras. They were all unnoticed. Unheralded. A weapon for the greater good.

"I'll tell you who *I* am," she said. "My great, great grandfather was a vampire. My great, great grandmother, after he left her, became a vampire hunter. Hunting has been in my family for generations, but I only recently found out. We don't hunt all of them, though, because not all vampires are bad. That's something you'll need to learn, if you want to win the game."

"That's a really rad character," said a woman three rows back.

"Sure," Arcadia said. *"Character."*

WATCHING, Nora said to her husband, "She's laying it on too thick."

JJ shook his head. "It's tried and true. I even ran it by Maurice."

"So now you're talking to Maurice?"

"When I can find him," JJ said. "He's a mite busy with the Council."

"Running for a seat?"

"Running for his life."

Nora hadn't heard about this. "Did something happen with his progeny? With Richard?"

"Reginald," JJ corrected. "And yes. It very much did."

"What?"

"He had his trial."

Nora had told herself she'd stay away from this topic. It made her want to punch things. After becoming a vampire and stepping back from the human world (JJ helped; she had a more flexible situation than he did and was actually able to visit her family), Nora had seen her life with new perspective. She realized how much she'd tolerated because she'd known no better. A million tiny insults and condescensions that'd previously been invisible were suddenly neon-sign obvious. She'd been passed over at work because they thought her too introverted and weird. People she thought were her friends were, with her new vampire insight, obviously making fun of her. Yet who had optimized all those interlinked databases without losing a single bit of information? Nora, of course. Jameson had taken the credit; Nora had been too shy to speak up. But that way was over. Nora was a new woman now.

Now that vampirism was working on her mind, her latent skills had doubled, quadrupled. What she'd been good at, she was suddenly *very* good at. She wasn't nearly as strong or (go ahead; say it) as attractive as the pretty-boy and pretty-girl vampires out there in the "approved" vampire world, but then again that's why Nora and Rohit hadn't let the Council know they existed. Technically, wanton creation was a crime in the eyes of the Council — and because of it, JJ was as much to blame for Nora's creation as Nora herself. Meanwhile news of Maurice Toussant's wanton creation was news all over the Vampire Nation — enough that even Nora couldn't block it out. JJ often gave her secret updates that nobody knew (such as the things Reginald Baskin could do — nobody but Maurice knew that), but only half of the time did "Reggie updates" inspire Nora. The rest of the time, the way he was treated triggered

Nora's own memories. Becoming vampire had given her a way to belong that she hadn't had before, but hearing about Reginald was just a reminder that if the wider vampire world knew she existed, even monsters would treat her the same.

"Well?" Nora asked. "Did he pass the trial?"

JJ actually laughed. "Dear God no. Come on, Nora. Nobody in the Nation even knows his name. They just call him 'the fat vampire.' Even if he'd performed well, he never had a chance."

Despite his words, JJ was smiling. It was maddening.

"What?" Nora asked.

"Aren't you going to ask what happened?"

She looked up to see Arcadia finishing her speech. She did the speech every time for what looked like no reason, but really it was just to let participants know once more that Blood Mayhem *understood*; Blood Mayhem knew these misfits like nobody else in their lives ever had.

Arcadia left the stage and kissed Amelie. Now that Arcadia's hair was back to its natural color, the two could have been twins. If they could have babies together, the babies from those two mothers would probably have looked like clones.

Orlo, because he was Orlo, still hadn't dropped his torch for Amelie. When asked, he kept saying, "You never know."

THE PLAYERS PLAYED. It didn't matter who lost, who won, or how they performed. The old Minerva Guild was watching for more subtle things from the players in their game: metrics that Maurice, before he'd had to go on the run, helped them create. Maurice, said JJ, worked for a fitness supply company. He'd been made before Logan-era restrictions and hence didn't fit the mold, either. From pictures JJ showed, the two-thousand-year-old vampire was maybe five-seven, skinny, and looked like a sixteen-year-old goth. Yet he was apparently a genius. So much, stored in that ancient mind of his.

"Look at this," said Brody, pointing at a camera view on of the many screens in front of him. "This is the deacon's lair." He tapped the screen right here. "This guy, 771 ..."

Beside him, Amelie looked up the number. "Victor Eli," she said.

"Rohit's in there along with some of our human volunteers. When they attacked, Rohit climbed onto the ceiling and ..."

Nora rolled her eyes. "I told him not to do that. Human beings can't do that."

"They'll assume it's special effects, *Nora*," said Brody, "like when you cut off your own face."

"That was an accident," Nora said.

"Anyway, Victor didn't even flinch. Wasn't scared at all."

"Because he thinks it's special effects," said Nora. She tapped the screen. "Is that JJ?"

Brody nodded. "He hasn't jumped out yet. They don't know he's there."

"He wearing an earpiece?"

Brody laughed as he looked up at her. "Does he need one?"

Now Nora laughed. Then she focused inside herself and reached out to him through the blood tie they shared.

JJ. Grab the girl about ten feet from you, then growl at the guy.

Onscreen, what looked like a pile of laundry erupted as JJ sprung from it. He did as Nora asked, grabbing the second person in the room and growling at the first. Still, Victor Eli didn't run.

Tell him that if he leaves now, you'll spare his life.

What about her? JJ asked back.

Tell him she dies anyway.

Onscreen, JJ did, but Victor Eli stood firm, ready to fight rather than leave his friend behind. Brody nodded appreciatively.

"He knows it's just a game," Arcadia said. "It might not mean anything."

"Really?" Nora asked, looking at Arcadia. "Was that why you risked your point lead to help us back in Detroit?"

"We lost Detroit," Arcadia said. "We both did."

"And yet, look at us now."

Brody nodded at that, then turned to Orlo, who was taking notes on his laptop. "Eli, Victor," he told Orlo. "Add him to the list."

AT DAY'S END, with the players gone and lists of potential follow-ups made, Nora found JJ sitting in the elbow of the building, outside opposite the setting sun. Long rays of orange light still kissed the building's long angles. They were slowly turning red. Sunset was minutes away.

She sat beside him.

"I don't like being out here when the sun is up," she said.

"It's almost down."

She shivered. "All that reflected radiation. I feel like I'm getting a burn just being here."

"Come on, Nora. Don't you miss the beauty?"

She just stared at him.

"You're supposed to say you already *have* beauty," he told her.

Still she said nothing.

"Because you have me," JJ explained.

"I know. It's not becoming, you fishing for compliments."

"I had a bad upbringing. My father was a murdering bastard."

"Your maker was not your father, JJ."

"Yeah, well, I never knew my father. He may have been a murdering bastard, too."

They sat until the sun was set. Then JJ rose, and Nora rose with him. There were no mercury vapor lights outside here. They looked for that sort of thing now, whenever they recruited.

"Good list today?" JJ asked.

"Low numbers, but good quality."

"Hunters?"

"We're vampires. Do we really want to train vampire hunters?"

JJ shrugged. "You were human for so long. I still can't believe you don't see us as a threat."

"Do you see Jews as a threat?"

"No."

"Muslims?"

"No."

"What about women, JJ? Some of us are out to cut off your balls."

"They'd just grow back," JJ said.

"You know what I mean," Nora said.

"No. I don't see women as a threat."

"There you go, then. Difference does not make an

enemy. Neither of us see *vampires* as a threat, either. Not simply because they're vampires, anyway."

"It's different," JJ said.

Nora stopped and turned her husband toward her. "It's not different. And with all the affection in the world, my love, you really need to grow the fuck up and stop hating yourself so much. I know our bodies can't change. I know I'll have no boobs forever. I asked, you know. I asked a vampire surgeon, more because I was curious than anything else. Do you know what would happen if I got boob implants?"

"Don't get boob implants."

"They'd pop right out," Nora said. "Like squeezing pills from bubble-pack."

"I love you how you are."

"Good. So maybe you should do the same."

He sighed. They'd been through this.

"My point is that our bodies can't change," Nora said. "You are like this forever. I am like this forever. And your friend Maurice's progeny? He'll be big forever. And so what? He can't catch prey. He can't seduce anyone. And yet you keep singing the praises of all the amazing things he can do."

"The things he can do are—"

Nora put a finger to JJ's lips to stop him. She could feel that his fangs had descended, and it turned her on a little.

"I know what he can do," she said. "Just like I know what you can do. Your past doesn't define you. Arek doesn't define you — not then, not now. He fooled you, and that sucked. He made you do terrible things." She shook her head. "It's embarrassing. Tragic. But it's not like you were simply *duped.* It was blood hypnosis, JJ, and you've atoned. *My God* have you atoned."

JJ made a noncommittal gesture. Nora went on.

"To answer your question, no, I don't really want to recruit hunters to go out there and stake vampires, but that's not because *we're* vampires. Not to be too pollyanna, but I don't want *anyone* out there hunting *anyone* solely on the basis of what they are."

"So it's the other plan."

She nodded. "They say you should be the change you want to see in the world. They say the only way to disrupt something is from the inside out."

"And you really think these kids want to be vampires?"

"They're not kids. None of them are under 25. We will speak to them one by one. Show them. Tell them every-thing. Our behavioral profiles are pretty good these days. It's unusual that I find someone we pre-screened as worthy in a game who isn't at least willing to listen. Not everyone hates this life, JJ. Once I got past the night-owl thing, I've found I like it just fine."

"You need to give them all the information. They need to make an informed—"

"—an informed decision," Nora said. "Yes, of course. I'll warn them away just like you want me to." She shook her head again. "Jesus, you sound like my mother."

They walked on.

"What's the point, Nora?"

"The Vampire Nation wants perfect vampires. I want misfits."

"Just to be an ass?"

"Every one of the misfits we identify through these games has a special skill, or ability, or trait," she told him. "When they turn, that trait magnifies. We're not making true misfits. It just looks that way to the Council."

"And when the Council catches them? When they're destroyed?"

"I'm not too worried about that," Nora said.

"Why?"

"Maurice. And, more importantly, this fat vampire of yours."

"They're on the run," JJ said.

"Yes. But look what they did in the meantime. How impossible was it supposed to be, JJ? How much did Reginald surprise them all? I heard he even—"

"Yes. He did."

"—even found a way to use his 'weakness' as a strength," Nora finished. The full story was more graphic than that, but including bloody details changed nothing.

JJ sighed. He'd learned to demur. If there'd ever been a time JJ thought he was in charge of this relationship, it was long gone now.

"That's what we do to beat them," Nora said. "We use what they think are weaknesses against them, as strengths."

"Sure."

"You don't agree?"

"I agree," he said. "It's just …"

"What?" But Nora knew this change in him. He'd let it go, and now he was just being an adorable asshole. She played along.

"It's just that I don't have any weaknesses," he said.

There was a copse of trees ahead, hidden in shade. Since becoming a vampire, Nora's libido had increased tenfold.

She pushed him toward the copse.

"Oh yes you do," she said.

The End

Not all vampires sparkle.

There's a war brewing in the vampire population. They've always lived beside us, but now they've been divided by a radical leader. In the modern age, there's no place for vampire misfits like the LARPers you just read about ... but one rebel, Maurice Toussant, has since made Reginald Baskin — a brand-new vampire stuck in a not-so-sparkly body. But what Reginald lacks in beauty and strength, he more than makes up for in wiles and intelligence. He might even be enough to bring down Logan's authoritative regime ... but that's just the beginning in Reginald's world-spanning battle between good and evil. Read Reginald's story — and that of the vampire revolution — in *Fat Vampire: The Complete Series* available now.

BUT WHAT ABOUT REGINALD?

If you're wondering what ended up happening with Reginald, his trial, and the future of Logan's elitist Vampire Nation, you might have missed out on my book **_FAT VAMPIRE_** — Reginald's story, which started it all!

Check out Fat Vampire (adapted in 2022 on the SyFy Network as Reginald the Vampire, starring Spider-Man's Jacob Batalon)!

YOU'VE TRIED VAMPIRES. NOW TRY
ZOMBIES.

***First things first. If you haven't read Fat
Vampire yet — the book that started all of this
— you should read that next FO SHO.***

Otherwise, I suggest **Dead City**: a biological thriller about
a zombie plague, the drug that stopped it and created a
fragile mixed human/zombie society, and how it all fell
apart ... maybe on purpose.

ENTER THE TRUANTVERSE

When it comes to stories and the worlds they live in, books are only the beginning.

Visit JohnnyBTruant.com/join to get my best books sooner and cheaper than the other stores.

My list doesn't suck like so many author email lists. Seriously. It has unicorns.

ALSO BY JOHNNY B. TRUANT

Winter Break

Pattern Black

Pretty Killer

Cursed

The Bialy Pimps

Namaste

The Target

La Fleur de Blanc

Axis of Aaron

Devil May Care

Screenplay

The Island

Burnout

Sick and Wired

UNICORN WESTERN:

Unicorn Western

The Wanderers

A Fistful of Magic

Shimmer to Yuma

The Man Who Shot Alan Whitney

The Spectacular Seven

Open Meadows

The Unforgotten

The Magic Bunch

Unicorn Genesis

FAT VAMPIRE:

Fat Vampire

Fat Vampire 2: Tastes Like Chicken

Fat Vampire 3: All You Can Eat

Fat Vampire 4: Harder Better Fatter Stronger

Fat Vampire 5: Fatpocalypse

Fat Vampire 6: Survival of the Fattest

The Vampire Maurice

Anarchy and Blood

Vampires in the White City

Fangs and Fame

Game of Fangs

INVASION:

Invasion

Contact

Colonization

Annihilation

Judgment

Extinction

Null Identity

COMEDIES:

Everyone Gets Divorced

Greens

Fiends

Decoy Wallet

NONFICTION:

The Fiction Formula

Fiction Unboxed

Iterate & Optimize

The Story Solution

Write. Publish. Repeat.

The One With All the Writing Advice

www.ingramcontent.com/pod-product-compliance
Lightning Source LLC
Chambersburg PA
CBHW032250310726
48973CB00008B/2357